The Secrets of Pond Street

second edition

written by: Robert Benson

illustrated by: Matthew McCosco

Copyright: by Robert D Benson, November 2011

Table of Contents

Chapter 1: A Cloud over Pond Street

Walking down the hill from where the school bus let her off, Karen Taylor was surprised to see her mother's car in the driveway. She ran the rest of the way home and burst into the front room, where her mother was busy at the kitchen sink. "Mom," she said, "what's wrong. Why are you home?"

Her mother did not turn around. Karen could not see the worried frown that passed over her face like a dark cloud across the sun. "I got the dinner shift off," she said brightly. "In fact, I'm going to get two nights a week off from now on, so I can come home and cook dinner like a normal mother. Won't that be nice?"

Karen's face broke into a delighted smile, but just as suddenly bunched into a puzzled frown. "But I thought you were going to ask Mr. Colston for more hours?"

"Well, yes ..." her mom sighed. "But if I got more hours, I'd just be taking them away from Brenda, and she needs the money just as much as we do. Mr. Colston decided there wasn't enough business for both of us on week nights, so he cut out two of my shifts and three of Brenda's."

"Does that mean we won't have enough money?"

"Don't worry about that," Mrs. Taylor said quickly. "I'll figure out something. Why don't you go out and play this afternoon? I'll take care of the garden."

"Oh, that's okay. I'll do it. I like working in the garden."

"I know, but I wish you'd go out and play with some of the kids on the street. It's a nice day, and you're alone too much ... since Eva moved away."

"I don't mind. I'm not really friends with any of the other kids on the street."

"That's what I'm talking about," her mother said, turning to Karen with a frown. "You need to go out and make friends. I know you miss Eva, but sometimes things happen that we can't control. We've all got to move on and make the best of things."

"I'm okay," Karen insisted, with just a trace of hardness creeping into her voice. "I don't mind being alone, and anyway, what about you? Dad died eight years ago and you haven't gone out on one date yet."

"Don't change the subject," Karen's mom said sharply. "I want you to go out and play this afternoon, and I don't want any back talk. Okay?"

Karen said, "Okay," but there was a dark stubborn look in her eyes that Mrs. Taylor had never seen before.

Karen went into her room and changed into jeans and hiking boots. She left the house without another word and walked up the street to where she could see four or five kids playing kickball - just the kind of game her mother would want her to get into. Instead of joining them, she turned and cut through a neighbor's yard into the woods, where she angled back down the hill to the path that ran from her own back yard through the swamp.

Her mother could throw her out of the house, but she couldn't tell her who her friends should be. Karen wasn't two years old, and that was something she had to decide for herself. Still, she was not used to disobeying her mother, and she was upset about it. She needed a good tromp in the woods to settle herself down.

Karen and her mother lived on Pond Street, in the small town of Pine Springs, in the low rolling foothills where the Rocky Mountains rise up out of the Great Plains. The town is nestled in the crook of a ridge that climbs steeply to the north. To the west, a valley leads up to a pass through snow-capped mountains. Runoff from melting snow feeds the springs that create a great marshy area to the east of town known as Skinner's Swamp. An interstate highway runs between the town and the swamp, then turns and runs up the valley to the pass. When the interstate was built, it cut off Pond Street from the rest of town, leaving it a dead-end street stuck between a four lane highway and a swamp.

Karen's house was at the very end of the street, where the giant pines of the swamp came right up to the back door. The house was small, just three rooms. Karen's room, her mother's room, and a tiny bathroom were squeezed into the back of the house. Across the front, there was one long room that included a kitchen, a table, and a living room area. The house was small and mossy in the shade of the pines, but it was cozy, and Karen liked being close to the woods.

Before Eva moved away, it was perfect. Eva had lived across the street for as long as Karen could remember. They were in the same grade in school and had been best friends forever, like sisters almost, only better. They did everything together and hardly ever fought. When Eva told Karen that her family had to move to California because her father had lost his job at the furniture factory, Karen felt like her world had fallen apart. Two weeks later, Eva was gone, and Karen had not seen her since.

Now, Eva's house sat empty across the street. The windows were dark and blank without their curtains. The grass was high and shaggy in the yard, and weeds had grown up through the front walk. The lopsided front porch had always looked kind of cute, before. Now, it made the house look like it was abandoned and kind of spooky. Karen shivered whenever she happened to look over there. It was a constant reminder that powerful and mysterious forces were loose in the world, forces that could suddenly drop into the middle of the happiest lives and scramble them into strange, ill-fitting pieces.

Karen was 12 years old, a skinny girl with light brown hair that she wore in long braids. She had big brown eyes with golden flecks that sparkled when she laughed. With Eva, she had always been open, funny, and full of ideas. At school, she was quiet, polite and reserved. Her clothes always looked old-fashioned, since they were usually the left-overs of previous seasons. The kids thought she was a brain, an oddball, and not very friendly.

Since Karen's father had died when she was four, her mother had struggled to support the two of them. She worked long hours at the diner in town, but the tips she brought home never seemed to be enough. The furniture factory was the only major industry in town, and it was losing business, cutting shifts and laying off workers. People couldn't afford to eat out very often, even at the diner. It seemed like the more hours Mrs. Taylor worked, the less money she made.

With her mom working all the time, Karen's duties (besides school and homework) were keeping the house clean and tending the little garden in the back yard. But even with her household responsibilities, she still had many hours free for "tromping" through the woods. Tromping was a funny word she and Eva had invented to describe their favorite activity – exploring the seemingly endless woods between the ridge and the swamp.

The only path through the swamp started in Karen's back yard. From there it was no more than half a mile to the other side of the swamp, where a steep slope led up to a broad, rocky plateau covered with scrub pine, the area that Karen called simply "the woods," though even that name may have been a little too grand. Except for the swamp, where it was too soggy for heavy equipment, the virgin forests had been stripped from the gently rolling terrain many years ago. The trees that grew back were stunted and useless for lumber. Deer were not interested in the brush that grew in tangled thickets, so the hunters didn't bother with this area either. It was just a big open wilderness that Karen had almost to herself.

With the ridge sticking up above the trees to the north, she always had a guide to get her home. She could lace up her hiking boots and strike out in any direction, pick her way over miles of rugged ground, and come right back to her house without a trail or a map. She loved the smell of the pines and the soft crisp feel of their needles under her feet. Before with Eva, and now alone, she had criss-crossed many square miles, discovering interesting rock formations, meadows, a little spring, and an old abandoned logging camp. Sometimes she saw porcupines, skunks, and other small animals. Once she had seen a fox loping across an open space. Even without Eva, the woods were special to her. Simple and quiet, it was a perfect place for sorting out the things on her mind.

One of those things was her ongoing argument with her mother. Mrs. Taylor kept pushing her to go out and make new friends. She didn't like Karen walking in the woods alone. But Karen wasn't interested in making new friends. She liked the solitude of the woods, and she wasn't the least bit afraid of it. Karen was devoted to her mother and usually did what she asked without question, but this was one area where they had a serious disagreement, and it bothered both of them.

That afternoon, Karen took the path through the swamp, then climbed the slope up into the scrub forest on the other side. The sun was shining and a soft cool breeze flowed down from the mountains. Birds chirped and squawked from the trees, but Karen didn't notice any of it. She walked with her head down, letting her feet find the way, deep in thought. It was nearly six o'clock when she came back to the path through the swamp. She had tromped several miles over rough and rocky terrain, without any path to smooth the way, but she wasn't tired.

As usual, the walk helped her to see her problem clearly. Her mother was just having trouble accepting the fact that Karen was growing up. She thought Karen still lived in a child's world of make-believe, where children "played" with other children. She couldn't understand that, for Karen, that world was gone. The morning Karen watched Eva waving goodbye from the back seat of her father's car as they drove away, that childhood world had changed. If the troubles at the factory and all that murky business of the adult world could reach right onto her street and pluck away her best friend, Karen could not just forget about it and go out and play. She had to take her place in that world. She had to work to protect what she loved and struggle to make her world the one she wanted to live in and believe in. That was what her mother didn't understand.

The sun was getting low over the mountains. The swamp was filling with shadow. As Karen approached her little house, she saw a light shining in the window. She glanced inside and saw her mother sitting at the table, staring down at some papers in front of her. Mrs. Taylor was only 35, but long hours of hard work and worry had worn her down. She had a beautiful oval face, framed by thick auburn hair, with a wide, generous mouth and gray-green eyes, but weariness lay over her features like a mask.

When Karen came in, her mother was stuffing the papers into a kitchen drawer. She turned to Karen with a tired smile. "Hi Sweetie. Better wash up. Dinner's almost ready."

She didn't ask Karen who she had played with or what she'd done, so Karen didn't have to tell her the story which she had so carefully planned. That was a relief. Karen wasn't comfortable with the half-truths in her story. But her relief was clouded by the worry that her mother must have something serious on her mind to forget to ask about Karen's afternoon, especially after she had made such a big deal about pushing her out of the house in search of new friends. Both Karen and her mother were unusually quiet through dinner that night.

Karen was lying in bed in the dark when she heard her mother go to bed. She wasn't sleepy, even though she had gotten up at six that morning and knew she'd be up at six again the next morning. She had more important things to do than sleep. She waited until no more sounds came from her mother's bedroom and then made herself wait fifteen minutes more before she got out of bed and padded silently into the front room. In deep darkness, Karen felt her way around the table into the kitchen area.

The drawer made a thin rubbing sound as she eased it open. Karen stopped and listened. Nothing disturbed the silence that seemed to hang heavily in the air. Karen reached into the drawer and pulled out the papers she had seen her mother put in there earlier. In the dark, all she could tell was that it was a loose stack of about 20 sheets stuffed into the

Karen saw her mother sitting at the table, staring
down at some papers

drawer on top of a folder of recipes Mrs. Taylor had clippedfrom old newspapers and magazines, but never had the time, or the right ingredients, to try.

Silently, Karen carried the papers back to her room and shut the door. Then she sat down at her little writing desk and switched on the lamp. A circle of bright light fell on the top sheet of the papers that she laid before her on the desk. Karen wasn't surprised by what it said, but it gave her a nervous, sick feeling just the same.

In pencil, Mrs. Taylor had written "Budget" at the top of the page. Underneath, there were two columns, one labeled "Income," the other "Expenses." There were only two entries under Income - "Job" and something called "SS." Under Expenses, there were more than a dozen entries, such as "Food," Clothing," "Electric," and "Mortgage." Each of these items had dollar amounts next to them. Many of the amounts listed as Expenses looked like they had been erased and changed, some several times. Both columns were added up at the bottom, and Karen could see immediately why her mother seemed so tired and withdrawn. No matter what changes she made to the entries in the Expenses column, Mrs. Taylor couldn't cut the total down enough to match the Income.

Chapter 2: Karen's First Job

Early the next morning, as the sun struggled down through the trees, Karen sat at the table eating her breakfast. The table was a heavy old piece of oak supported on thick wooden legs. It stood in the middle of the front room, separating the kitchen area from the living room. From where she sat, Karen could look out through the window to the street and Eva's house on the other side. Her mom was hustling around the kitchen, packing Karen's lunch and checking her homework.

"Mom," Karen said solemnly, "I want to get a job. Maybe I can make enough money to help."

Mrs. Taylor smiled. "Sweetie, that's nice, but you're too young."

"Why? Tommy Ryan is a paperboy. Why couldn't I do that?"

"Tommy Ryan is fourteen and his father works for the paper. Besides, your job is school. Remember? You've got to get good grades and go as far as you can with your education so you can do great things when you grow up."

"That's too long to wait," Karen protested. "I want to help now."

"I know you do, Sweetheart, but you can't. I'd rather you spent some time with the other kids on the street. You should be having fun. Let me worry about the money." Her mother tried to smile confidently, but Karen could see she was scared.

Her mother just didn't get it. Karen knew she was old enough to help. That afternoon, after school, she went up and down Pond Street, asking anyone who came to the door if they had any chores she could do. Most of them said no and shut the door with a sad and worried look in their eyes. Some laughed and said they had lots of chores, but they couldn't pay her to do them.

She even knocked at old Mr. Vandergaard's door, although his reputation made her a little nervous. Mr. Vandergaard lived a few doors up the street on the other side. His house was the first one built on Pond Street, before there was even a street there. The old man had lived there longer than anyone else on the street, but he kept to himself. People on the street often saw him out walking with his dog. He would nod and say hello when they passed, but that was all. He didn't seem to want to stop and talk, and no friends or family came to visit him. Karen had seen him out around the neighborhood, and like many of the other people on the street, she had said hello and received a polite but uninviting reply. She was worried that he would be angry at her for breaking into his privacy, but she was determined to do everything she could to find work.

Mr. Vandergaard answered her knock wearing overalls over a long sleeve jersey, with reading glasses perched on the end of his nose. He was very old, but it was clear that he was once strong and fit. He stood very erect, almost six feet tall, but he moved slowly and carefully, as if his joints were stiff. His eyes were a muddy blue and his hair was white and thin. His dog, a big reddish brown mutt with a shaggy head and a white muzzle, came up behind him and woofed once, looking out through the screen door at Karen.

"Quiet Barney," Mr. Vandergaard said to the dog, who promptly lay down and paid no more attention to either Karen or his master. "Yes?" the old man said to Karen in a cool, polite voice.

"Hello, Mr. Vandergaard. I'm Karen Taylor from just down the street." Karen pointed vaguely toward her house.

"Yes, I know. You're Elaine Taylor's girl. What can I do for you?"

"Well, I'm looking for work. I thought you might have some kind of chores I could do. I'm pretty good at cleaning and gardening, and I wouldn't charge very much. Do you have anything like that?"

Mr. Vandergaard took off the glasses and rubbed his nose thoughtfully. He frowned, but it wasn't threatening, more apologetic. "I don't think so, Karen. See, if I didn't have the chores for myself, I wouldn't have anything to do. There's only so much reading I can do, and old Barney doesn't like to walk too far, anymore. Sorry."

"Oh, that's okay. Nobody else has anything, either," Karen admitted ruefully. "Thanks anyway. It was nice talking to you."

"Good luck," he said. "It was nice talking to you, too." Karen was surprised at Mr. Vandergaard. He didn't seem unfriendly at all. But she was discouraged at her lack of success. After knocking on every door on the street, she had found exactly nothing. There was only one more house to try, her next door neighbors, the Gundersons. Mr. Gunderson was blind, so his wife had to do most of the work around the house, but Karen's mother said they lived on a fixed income, which apparently meant they had to watch every penny. She didn't think they would have anything, but it couldn't hurt to ask.

Mrs. Gunderson came to the door and Karen explained what she wanted.

"Oh dear," the old lady said, "I wish there was something I could do, but we don't have any money for that."

"I understand," Karen said. "Nobody does. Well, thank you anyway."

"Good luck, dear. I'm so sorry."

Karen started across the weedy yard toward her house. "Wait, Karen," Mrs. Gunderson called. "Maybe there is something."

When Karen turned back, the old lady had come out on the front step. "I've been having trouble reading to Mr. Gunderson," she said softly, as if she was afraid that someone would overhear. "My eyes aren't so good anymore. I ... I couldn't pay you very much, but I know he'd feel a lot better if someone could read to him."

"I could do that," Karen said eagerly.

"I think I could give you a dollar a day if you could read to him in the afternoon."

It wasn't much, but it was something. "That would be wonderful," Karen said enthusiastically.

"Alright, dear," Mrs. Gunderson said, smiling and putting a finger to her lips. "When would you like to start?"

"This afternoon, if that's alright."

Mrs. Gunderson brought Karen into the room she called the parlor. The small room was crammed with rickety old tables and shelves. There were pictures, embroidery, and lace on the walls, with figurines, and little decorative bowls resting on every surface. It seemed very crowded to Karen and gave the room a stuffy overheated feeling. Two old-fashioned, high-backed, stuffed chairs stood on either side of the window that looked out to the street. Karen sat on one of them while Mrs. Gunderson went to get her husband.

As Karen looked around, she noticed that one of the pictures on a carved wooden shelf showed a younger Mr. and Mrs. Gunderson with another couple on the deck of a big sailboat plowing through a bright blue-green sea. Mr. Gunderson had his hands on a big metal wheel, apparently steering the boat. All of them were smiling and waving at the camera. Karen had never even seen the ocean. She wondered briefly how this poor old couple had ever happened to be out on that boat.

She heard loud whispers coming from the bedroom, but couldn't catch the words. It might have been her imagination, but it sounded like Mr. Gunderson was angry about having Karen read to him. His wife stood firm until Karen heard him say: "Alright, but I'm not an invalid. I can still take care of myself."

"Oh, pish," Mrs. Gunderson said, "nobody ever said you were an invalid."

She came into the room with Mr. Gunderson holding her arm, shuffling alongside her. He was frail and slightly bent, moving slowly. His thin white hair let the freckles on his scalp show through. His eyes were open, but didn't focus on anything. He wore heavy wool socks and slippers, and a bathrobe over his pants and shirt. "Hello, Karen," he said in a kindly voice, but his eyes wandered helplessly around the room.

"Hello, Mr. Gunderson."

Mrs. Gunderson brought him to the other stuffed chair. "You sit there, Papa. Now what should I get for Karen to read you?"

The old man frowned. "Well," he said gruffly, "if I could see, I'd be reading my *Business Week*."

"Oh, now Hal. I don't think Karen could read something like that."

"Sure I can," Karen said quickly. "I'm a good reader. I might not understand it, but that's okay. After all, I'm not reading for myself."

Mr. Gunderson turned to her and smiled. "Thank you, Karen. I can help with any words you don't know."

Mrs. Gunderson wasn't convinced, but she brought the magazine. "If you have any trouble with this, Karen, I can bring you something else. Mr. Gunderson is just being stubborn."

Karen read the names of the articles from the table of contents and Mr. Gunderson picked one out. When Karen found it and started reading, she thought maybe she had promised more than she could deliver. There were words and abbreviations in the article that she had never seen before. She had to sound out the words and repeat the abbreviations without any idea what they meant. She got through the article but didn't understand it at all. Mr. Gunderson smiled a couple times when she stumbled over strange words, but he thanked her when she finished and asked if she'd read another. Karen ended up reading half the magazine, staying until the weak sunlight in the trees began to fade. She wanted to get home to do some weeding in the garden while there was still a bit of daylight to work with. Mr. Gunderson had fallen asleep as she read the last article anyway.

Mrs. Gunderson gave her a dollar bill as she left. "Thank you, dear," she said. "It means so much to him, you know. Please come again tomorrow if you can."

"Oh I'll be here," Karen said, smiling and holding the dollar tightly in her hand. "Thank you so much."

Mr. Gunderson

Karen raced through her chores and finished her homework just before it was time for her mother to get home. She cleared her books and papers and put the dollar bill in the middle of the table, where her mother couldn't fail to see it. Then she went into the bedroom grinning at her little surprise.

She heard her mother come in, open and close the refrigerator, then slump heavily into her chair at the table. "Huh?" she said. "What's this? Karen?"

Karen came out with a sheepish look on her face. "Mom, I know you said not to, but I got a job today. That's my pay. Don't worry, I got all my homework done too," she added quickly.

"But Karen, what kind of job did you get?"

"Reading to Mr. Gunderson. Mrs. Gunderson's eyes are too weak. And it was hard, too, because I had to read a business magazine that I didn't understand, but he liked it, and Mrs. Gunderson said she would give me a dollar every day if I'd come over and read to him. I know it's not much, Mom, but it's something, isn't it? It will help a little, won't it?"

Mrs. Taylor looked down at the dollar and suddenly burst into tears.

Karen was shocked. "Mom, what's wrong?"

Karen's mother cried silently for a minute, then raised her face to her daughter. "How did you know?" she asked, shaking her head.

"Know what?"

"How bad we need the money."

"I don't know," Karen lied. "Just all the things we can't have."

"But it's worse than that, Sweetheart. I just found out today. The bank wants all the back payments we owe on the house. They're going to take it away if I can't pay by the end of next month. There's no way I can get that money." She picked up the dollar and stared at it until the tears came again. "It's like you knew."

Karen came around the table and put an arm across her mother's back. "Don't worry, Mom. We'll figure something out."

"How? What I make isn't enough to support us, and now I won't even be making that much. I've got to see if I can get another job or a loan or something."

"Something will work out," Karen said confidently. "We'll be okay."

That night, Karen wrote to Eva. Every Saturday morning, Karen went to the town library and used their computer to send a long e-mail to Eva, but she wrote things to put in the e-mail whenever she had something to say. During the week, these notes were more like a diary, recording the things that were bubbling up out of her head at the time. Writing them down, it felt like she was talking them over with Eva just like they had always done. Eva loved to get the e-mails, but she wasn't as good about writing back. Her replies were short and awkward, and there wasn't much about what she was doing. That didn't stop Karen from writing, though. If anything, she just became more determined than ever to keep up their communication. Eva was too good a friend to lose, and anyway, the very act of writing down her thoughts helped her make sense of them. That night, she sat at her little desk, where the lamp shed a soft circle of yellow light around her notebook, and wrote:

Now I know how you felt when you had to move away. I think Mom and I are in the same kind of trouble. The bank says they're going to take away our house if we can't pay them a lot of money, and we can't. Mom works all the time at the diner, but it's not enough. I even got a job reading to Mr. Gunderson. Mom didn't want me to, but I kind of disobeyed her and did it anyway. At least when she found out, she didn't say no. But I don't think the money I make is going to help very much. I don't want to leave our house – unless we could move to California where you are. Is it better there? Do you have a nice house? Can your parents afford it? This money problem is really bad.

On top of that, my mom is always nagging at me to go out and play with the other kids on the street. How can she think about playing at a time like this? She thinks I'm still just a kid, and maybe I am, but now I've got to grow up and help somehow. What do you think I should do?

Chapter 3: Mr. Gunderson

The next day, Karen was unusually gloomy and quiet when she went next door to read to Mr. Gunderson. She read from an old *Wall Street Journal*, and saw many of the same strange words she had encountered the day before, along with several new ones. Mr. Gunderson helped her with the pronunciations, but he didn't try to explain what they meant, and Karen didn't care. Her thoughts were far from the dry business news she was reading until a crazy idea entered her head. She read through the whole paper, skipping the articles that Mr. Gunderson didn't want. When she was through, Mr. Gunderson took a dollar from his shirt pocket and gave it to her.

"You really deserve more, Karen. You're a very good reader and you really brighten my day. We just can't afford any more."

"I know. That's alright. It's hard to get any kind of job at my age."

"Around here it's getting hard for people at any age."

Karen was quiet for a moment, thinking. Finally, she asked, "Mr. Gunderson, why do you like to read about business?"

The old man smiled. His eyes pointed over her head as if they could see something very far away. "I used to be part of it," he said. "I suppose it's foolish now that I'm not, but I always thought it was interesting and exciting and I guess I still do."

"So you know a lot about money and business and stuff like that?"

"More than most people, I guess."

"Can they really take a person's house away because they're behind on payments?" It came out in a sudden rush, not at all the way Karen intended, but once she started, she couldn't hold back.

Mr. Gunderson frowned. His soft unfocused eyes searched unsuccessfully for Karen's face. "Well, yes they can, but the banks don't like to do it, so it doesn't happen very often," he said slowly.

"But where do the people go?"

Mr. Gunderson's frown softened into a sad smile. "That's a good question. I guess that's really the most important question, isn't it? Well, if they have enough money, they might be able to find a cheaper place to buy or rent. Sometimes the government can help. Or they might just be homeless. You've heard about homeless people, right?"

"Yes, but I thought they were all crazy or on drugs or something."

"Sometimes, but more and more, they're just people who can't afford a home."

"Oh," Karen said softly, as the worried look returned to her face.

When Karen came back from the Gunderson's Mrs. Taylor was already home, cooking soup for supper and doing the breakfast dishes that Karen hadn't had a chance to do.

"Sorry, Mom," she said, "After school I had to go right over to read to Mr. Gunderson."

"That's alright. Now that I've got a couple nights off, I can do a little more around here." She didn't turn from the sink, but the corners of her mouth curled up in a small smile. "And with you working and all ..."

Karen was laying out her homework on the table. "Oh, right. Here's my dollar." She fished the crumpled bill out of the pocket of her jeans and brought it to her mother, who took it with wet soapy fingers.

"I'm going to put all your pay in a jar in the cupboard, so we can watch it add up."

"Great. Then we can use it to pay the bank next month."

"Right, but we're going to need a lot more than that, I'm afraid."

"How much?"

"$3,000."

"That much?" Karen groaned. "We can't pay that much, can we?"

Her mother turned to Karen. She looked tired and serious, but not defeated. "No, we can't," she said.

"Then what'll we do? Can we rent another house?"

"I don't know, honey. Maybe if we pay part of it, the bank will let us stay here. I'm going to try to talk to Mr. Wilson down at the bank tomorrow."

"Good. Mr. Gunderson says they don't take away people's houses very often."

"Karen," said Mrs. Taylor sharply, "were you talking to Mr. Gunderson about our problems?"

"No. But he knows a lot about business and things. I just asked him if the bank could really do that, not about us."

"That's private business, Karen. I'm trusting you with grown-up information because it affects you and you deserve to know, but it's not something we should be talking about with our neighbors. Okay?"

"Yes, Mom, but maybe Mr. Gunderson could help. I'm sure he would if he could."

"No, Sweetheart. I know Mr. Gunderson would like to help, but money things are private. You just don't talk about them, even with people you know and trust."

"Why not?" Karen asked. She wasn't disagreeing. It was more like curiosity about something she didn't understand.

"Well, it prevents problems. It's considered bad manners, like bragging."

Karen still looked puzzled. "How could it be bragging when we're in such a mess?"

"I know, but then it's like complaining. That's no good either."

"I didn't mean it that way."

"Of course not, honey, but that's the thing about money. It's such a touchy subject, people can take it wrong."

"I guess," Karen said, but she didn't sound convinced.

Karen's pay jar

Chapter 4: The Man in the Woods

On Saturday, Karen's mother went to work early. She would not be home until well after dark. As soon as it opened, Karen rode her bike to the library and sent off her weekly email to Eva. After lunch, she had some time before she had to go next door to read to Mr. Gunderson. She put on her hiking boots and went out past the garden, through the swamp, and into the forest. She hadn't thought about where she would go. She just wanted to be out in the woods, moving with the old familiar tromping rhythm. She let her feet find the way, as her thoughts struggled through the worrisome problems that seemed to have sprung up all around her.

It was a warm spring day, and the woods were at their very best. The smell of the trees and the little green shoots poking up through the carpet of pine needles was clean and fresh. The sun was bright in a cloudless sky, gently warming the air. Birds and insects sang all around her, but Karen noticed none of it. She was lost in an unfamiliar world of banks, laws, jobs and money, all of them looming over her little house like a tornado, ready to snatch it away forever.

But as soon as she thought of the little house, she couldn't help but think of the face she'd seen in pictures a thousand times, the face of a young man with dark hair and laughing eyes, the face of a person she'd seen so long ago that the memory might have been nothing more than a dream - the face of her father. But as vague and ghostly as that face was to Karen, she knew it was as solid and real as flesh and blood to her mother. So many things came up in their day to day lives that reminded Mrs. Taylor of her dead husband. A soft sad smile would come over her face when she stopped to point them out to Karen, saying: "your father chose this spot for the garden," or "your father put that patch on the roof," or "your father and I used to sit right here on the front step and watch the sunset," or a thousand other things that her father had done. It seemed as if her mother was trying to make that young man from the pictures as real to Karen as he was to her. And Karen tried too. Sometimes she shut her eyes very tight and tried to see that young man laugh, tried to hear his voice, tried to feel the bristles of his beard as she imagined him bending down to kiss her good night – but nothing she could do would make it real. When she opened her eyes, he was gone. Second-hand memories from her mother could not fill that void.

While Karen's imagination was straining to recreate her father, her feet were carrying her effortlessly through the forest, tracing a great circle. She was almost back to the High Road through the swamp when she suddenly looked up and saw a young man standing not more than twenty feet away beside a low outcropping of rock. The man wore blue jeans and a reflective vest over a black T-shirt. There was some kind of radio or telephone hooked to his belt. He was staring at Karen with a mocking grin on his face, and he was holding an upright pole stuck into the ground that was as tall as him. Karen stopped in her tracks and let out a little cry of surprise and confusion. At first, the young man seemed like the dream of her father come to life. He had the same laughing eyes. But she stared for a moment and saw that he didn't really look much like the pictures. He had lighter hair and a wider face.

"Hello," the young man said, his smile turning open and friendly.

"Um, hello," Karen said uncertainly. "What are you doing here?"

The young man laughed. "Funny, that's what I was going to ask you."

"I'm just taking a walk."

"Oh," the man said. "That's nice. Well, I'm just working."

"Working? Doing what?"

He laughed again and pointed to the pole. "I'm holding the stick."

"That's work?" Karen didn't mean to be insulting, but it might have come out that way.

The man didn't seem to mind. He laughed. "I know. I get to walk around in the woods, hold the stick and get paid for it. Doesn't seem right, does it."

"No. I mean, who pays you?"

He pointed off in the distance, and Karen saw another man on the far side of a shallow ravine. The man was looking at them through a little telescope. "That's my boss," the young man said. "We're making a kind of map of this place."

"Why?"

"I don't know," he shrugged. "Somebody wants it and they're willing to pay for it."

"Who would want a map of these woods? I walk around here all the time and I never see anybody."

"Whoever it is, I don't think they want the map to find their way. They're probably trying to sell this property."

"How do you know that?"

"That's what it usually is." The man looked thoughtful. "You say you come out here a lot?"

"Yeah."

"What about that swamp?"

"Skinner's Swamp? What about it?"

"You see people down there much?"

"Never." Karen made a face. "You step in the wrong place down there and you're in mud up to your knees."

"All year 'round?"

"Well, not winter. It freezes."

"Right. But it never dries up?"

"No."

Suddenly the radio thing on the man's belt squawked. "Ron, hold it straight," a tinny voice commanded. "Is it plumb?"

The young man looked at a little gauge on the pole and unhooked the radio. "I've got it," he said into the speaker. "Plumb."

"Okay. Now, get up on that rock behind you and stay on the same line."

"Got it," he said. He picked up the pole and turned to Karen with a smile. "Well, back to work. Hey, what's your name? I'm Ron."

"I'm Karen."

"It was nice talking to you, Karen. Bye."

"Bye," Karen said, watching him scramble up the outcropping of rock.

Chapter 5: Davey

That afternoon, Karen told Mr. Gunderson about meeting Ron, the young man in the woods. The old man, who had been nodding comfortably through the last few articles, suddenly perked up. His eyes looked out into the distance, bright and alert, even if they couldn't see.

"That man and his boss were surveyors," he said, though he seemed distracted.

"Who would want to buy that land out there?" Karen asked. "There aren't even any roads."

"They could build the roads." Mr. Gunderson said, but he sounded almost like he was talking to himself.

"But why? Wouldn't it be easier to build in town?"

"That depends." Mr. Gunderson continued to think for a moment, then asked, "Mrs. Gunderson told me there's been a 'For Sale' sign on a house up the street. I think it's been there for months."

"Oh yeah. That's Davey Torvald's house. He told some of the kids at school his family might have to move away because they cut his father's hours at the factory."

"Mrs. Gunderson said they took the sign away a couple days ago. Did you hear if they sold it?"

"No. I don't know."

"Do you think you could find out?"

"Sure, I'll just ask Davey on Monday at school."

"Good," Mr. Gunderson said. "And if they did sell it, it would be interesting to know who bought it. With business off at the factory, somebody could be doing some speculating, trying to take advantage of people who are having money problems. But don't be too nosy. People get funny about that kind of thing."

Karen nodded. "I know."

Karen didn't go straight home when she left the Gundersons'. Instead, she walked up the street to the Torvald's house, which was a little bigger and a little nicer than her own. It had a second floor, and the kitchen, dining room and living room were all separate rooms. It even had a real garage, instead of a tin shed roof for a carport. Despite the extra room, Karen liked her house better because they weren't so close to the highway. When she got to the Torvalds' house, she could hear the cars and trucks whizzing by just a hundred yards away.

She also found that Mr. Gunderson was right. The sign that had been stuck in the front yard since the middle of the winter was gone, but it didn't look like the Torvalds had moved out. A car was parked in the driveway, and there were curtains in the windows. Maybe they just gave up on selling the house, like the bank had given up on selling Eva's.

The Meadowlark School was a single story brick building at the edge of town. Behind the school, the playground was a flat open field of close cropped weeds. On Monday, Karen found Davey Torvald on the playground at recess. He was playing kickball and his team was kicking, which meant he was standing around talking to a couple other boys, waiting for his turn at the plate. Karen stood at the edge of the playing field, pretending to watch the game.

Davey was popular. He was good at sports, friendly, and cute. Everybody knew him and looked up to him. Lots of the girls had secret crushes on him, and most of the boys wanted to be like him. Davey was a 7th grader, a year ahead of Karen, and he was in a group of all boys. There was no way she could just walk up to him and pull him out of his group to talk to her. She'd be teased and laughed right off the playground. On the other hand, Davey had second lunch and Karen had first, and she rarely ran into him after school. This might be the only chance she'd have to talk to him that day. She waited and watched.

There was a boy on first base and the next boy up kicked the ball into right field, sending the runner to third. One of the boys with Davey went to the plate, the other went out to third base to coach the runner. Davey stood alone, cheering and watching the game. Karen moved up to stand near him, as if she too was cheering and wanted a closer view. She was only two steps away, but he hadn't noticed her at all.

"Davey," she said, just loud enough for him to hear.

"Huh?" Davey looked at her blankly.

"I need to talk with you," she whispered. "It's important."

"No," he said, edging away, "I'm busy." But then his curiosity overcame his pride. He frowned and whispered back without looking at her: "Why? What's so important?"

"We can't talk here. Meet me after school down by the gym. Okay?"

Davey looked around to see if any of his friends had noticed he was talking to Karen. All the other boys were watching the game, jumping around and yelling. "I might have things to do," he whispered fiercely.

"This is more important," Karen insisted.

"Okay, okay. Just leave me alone. I'll be there, but this better be good."

When she heard the final bell, Karen jumped up and ran out of her classroom. She was the first one into the hall, but the other kids were right behind her, laughing, running, eager to get out of there. Karen hurried along with them down the hall, but suddenly turned aside into the alcove where big double doors led into the gym. She shuffled aimlessly back and forth in front of the doors and watched the kids streaming past. Twice she took a drink from the water fountain so that it wouldn't be obvious she was waiting to meet someone, but she didn't need to. None of the other kids noticed her standing there.

Suddenly, the hall was quiet. A few stragglers shuffled by, and then Davey appeared, coming out of the library. He walked toward her down the hall without looking at her. When he was almost to the alcove, he casually glanced up and down the hall before suddenly turning to push his way through the doors into the gym.

"Come on," he said harshly, still not looking at her.

Karen followed.

There was no one in the gym. The lights were off, so the only light was from a row of windows up near the ceiling. Just to their left as they came in, the bleachers had been pulled out for some event. Davey led her around to the far side of the seating, where they would be at least partially hidden from anyone coming into the gym. Even though they both tried to walk softly, their footsteps seemed to echo in the big open space.

"What do you want?" Davey demanded in an angry whisper.

"Your house," Karen whispered back, "it was for sale, right?"

"So?"

"Now the sign's gone. Did you sell it?"

"None of your business."

"I just want to make sure you don't get fooled."

"What do you mean - 'fooled'?"

"It's some kind of speculating," Karen said. She hoped the big unfamiliar word would sound as mysterious to Davey as it did to her. She took a deep breath and plunged into her story. "Some guy is going around taking advantage of people with money problems. It's awful for the people he fools."

"That's crazy. He'd be in jail."

"They keep trying to catch him, but he's too smart. He's got lawyers and everything."

Davey's frown was no longer angry. Now it was mostly worried. "What can the people do?" he asked.

"Well, it's only a problem if they sign some papers about selling. Your parents probably didn't do that, right?"

"I don't know. I think they signed something. We're supposed to be selling the house this summer. They said it's all set. You think this guy could be tricking them?"

"I don't know. Do you know who they're selling it to? Maybe I could find out if it's that guy."

"I don't know the guy's name," Davey said, thinking hard, "Mr. Wilson down at the bank arranged everything. But there was something funny about it. Mr. Wilson said the man was buying our house for his business, so it was the name of the business that was on all the papers."

"What was the name of the business? Do you remember?"

"Something Something Trust, I think. Ha, what a joke," Davey said bitterly. "The guy's going around tricking people and he calls his business a trust – like 'trust me.' Right."

"Wait. We don't know if it's the same guy. Why don't you see if you can find out the name of whoever's buying your house? I'll see if I can get the name of the guy that's pulling these tricks. Okay?"

"Yeah."

"Good. We'll see what we've got tomorrow. But for now, don't tell anybody. We don't want to scare the guy off. Maybe we can catch him in the act."

"Right."

Now Davey was excited, too. Karen was partly proud and partly ashamed. She was a nobody, but she had managed to get what she wanted from one of the most popular kids in the school. The fact that she had to stretch the truth to do it, while Davey had reacted openly and honestly, somehow turned the victory on its head and made her feel like the loser.

Chapter 6: Big Questions

Mr. Gunderson did not seem at all surprised when Karen told him what Davey had said. "It's a trust," he told her, "because they don't want anyone to know who it's for. If we dug down to see who runs it, all we'd find would be some lawyers and bankers."

"Why do they want Davey's house?" Karen asked.

Mr. Gunderson smiled off into space. "That's the big question, isn't it? But I'll bet it has something to do with those surveyors you saw in the woods."

Karen was silent for a moment, trying to understand. "How?" she finally asked.

"That's another good question, but if I'm right, it tells us one thing."

"What's that?"

"Whatever they're planning out there is big."

"Oh."

Karen sounded a little lost, so Mr. Gunderson explained. "Let's say they were planning to build some kind of business out there, something that would employ a lot of people in this town. They can buy up the houses here for almost nothing and then sell them for a big profit when the new business is announced. That happens sometimes around a big business development project."

"You mean they don't want to live in Davey's house?"

"I doubt it. That's what I was talking about when I said someone might be speculating."

Karen couldn't suppress a guilty laugh.

"What?" Mr. Gunderson asked.

"That's what I told Davey."

Karen's mother had to work late that night. When she got home, she seemed tired and sad. She sat with her shoulders slumped, silent, staring down at her hands folded in front of her on the table. Karen tried to cheer her up with small talk, but her mother barely answered. She couldn't remember ever seeing her mother this down. Karen began to get worried. Finally, she asked, "What's the matter, Mom?"

Her mother looked up, and her cheeks and forehead were all clenched tight, trying to hold back tears. "Oh, darling," she said, "I don't know what we're going to do, where we're going to live. They're going to kick us out."

"Why? What happened?"

The tears broke free and ran down her mother's cheeks. "I didn't want to tell you. I didn't want you to worry, but I guess you'll have to know."

"What?"

"I went to the bank today. I always thought we could borrow more money on the house. I didn't want to. It's hard enough to pay the little bit we owe each month as it is. But I couldn't think what else to do." Mrs. Taylor paused, choking back a sob.

"The bank wouldn't give you any money?" Karen guessed.

"No. Mr. Wilson said with what we owe and my income going down, the bank couldn't loan us anything."

"But what about the house?" Karen asked. "Isn't that worth something?"

"That's the problem. Mr. Wilson said there's no market for real estate with the factory closing down shifts and everything. They can't loan money based on property anymore."

"But what about ..." Karen stopped.

"... the Torvalds' house?" her mother finished for her. "Mr. Wilson said that showed just how bad the market is. They had it for sale for six months and reduced the price twice. Nobody even looked at it. Finally, they just gave up and took it off the market."

"They did?"

Mrs. Taylor was too upset to notice her daughter's confusion. She fumbled in her purse and pulled out a business card. She put the card on the table and stared at it with a troubled expression. "This might be our only hope," she said.

"What is it?" Karen asked.

"Mr. Wilson said there are companies that buy houses at very low prices, when nobody else wants them. I said I didn't want to sell, but he gave me this card anyway. If worse comes to worst, I can call this man and see what kind of price he'll give us."

"Don't do that, Mom," Karen said urgently.

"I don't want to, darling, but we might have to. I don't know what else to do."

"You could talk to Mr. Gunderson," Karen pleaded. "He reads about business all the time. I'm sure he could tell us what to do."

"I know, but we can't ask him to get involved in our private business. Besides, Mr. Wilson said it was important to keep quiet about this." She picked up the business card. "If more people in town heard about it, they'd all be calling this number."

"We've got to think of something else."

Karen's mother sighed and dropped the card on the table. "I hope so. We've still got a few weeks before we have to decide."

Karen picked up the card. The man's name was Gerard S. Bellamy. He was a managing partner for the Townsend Investment Trust.

Before she got into bed, Karen sat at her desk and wrote:

> Eva, there's something funny going on here. I saw some guys on the other side of the swamp making a map of the woods. Mr. Gunderson says it must be because someone wants to buy that land. Nobody knows who, or why, but it might have something to do with the people that are buying Davey Torvald's house. It's all a big secret, and it doesn't make any sense, but I'm going to figure it out.
>
> I wish you were here to help. But maybe you can anyway. Whatever happened to your house? It had a For Sale sign in front for a long time but now the sign is gone. Did you sell it or something? E-mail me soon, and tell me what you know. This could be important.

She didn't tell Eva about her private talk with Davey, even though she knew that, to Eva, that would be a big deal. Karen still felt guilty about the way she got his cooperation, and anyway, Eva would try to make it into something it wasn't. Karen didn't want to get into that.

Chapter 7: Secrets and Lies

The next day at recess, Davey told his friends he couldn't play kickball. He had things to do. Karen was standing near the jungle gym when he walked past. He wore an angry frown and did not look at her. His upper lip was swollen and cut. Without a word, Karen followed at a safe distance, far enough back so that no one would connect them. Davey disappeared around a corner of the building, and Karen quickly did the same.

"What did you find out," she asked eagerly when they were both out of sight of the playground.

"Nothing," Davey said, still scowling. "I tried to talk to my mom, to see if I could get a name out of her, but my dad heard me and went ballistic. He'd kill me if he knew I was talking to you about it, but I don't care. I hate him."

"Did he do that?" Karen asked, pointing to Davey's split lip.

"This?" Davey touched it gently. His scowl deepened and he turned away. "No. I fell down playing kickball last night."

"Oh. That's too bad."

"It's nothing," Davey said, shaking off his anger. "What do we do now?"

"I don't know. We still need that name. Did you ever see it or hear it?"

"Yeah, I did. I saw the papers once, right after they signed them, but I can't remember it now."

"Do you think you could remember if you heard it again?"

"Maybe."

"Was it Townsend Investment Trust?"

Davey's eyebrows shot up in surprise. "That's it. How did you know?"

"I talked to my mom last night. She must have heard it at the diner. What about Gerard S. Bellamy?"

"I don't know. Maybe him too. But that Townsend Investment Trust – that's it."

"Townsend Investment Trust," she told Mr. Gunderson that afternoon. "Somebody named Gerard S. Bellamy - they're the ones that bought Davey's house."

"Townsend Investment Trust ... Bellamy" he said slowly. "Davey got all that from his parents?"

"I guess," Karen said uncomfortably. "Maybe he just remembered it."

"Huh. Never heard of them, but that doesn't mean anything."

"Do you think they'd try to buy other people's houses around here?"

"I'd be surprised if they didn't. Why, did you hear about more?"

"Well, not exactly, but there could be. Maybe they bought Eva's house across the street. There's lots of people who don't have enough money anymore."

"That's true, and that's exactly what they're counting on. They take advantage of people who don't think they have any other choice."

"You mean they cheat them?"

Mr. Gunderson frowned. "It's not cheating, exactly, but they know about the development project, and the people whose houses they're buying don't. If the property values go up because of the project, they make a lot of money. It's not quite fair that the people who owned the property before don't get any of that money, but it's not quite cheating, either."

"What if the people don't sell their houses?"

"If they wait and sell them after the project starts, then they might get some of that money, too. Or, maybe the project doesn't happen, and nobody makes any money."

"So what should people do?"

"That depends. The one thing they should do is find out everything they can about the value of their property, and that means finding out about any new development that might happen around them."

"You mean like the project in the woods."

"Exactly."

"Then we've got to tell them."

"Yes," Mr. Gunderson said slowly, "but I think we should know a little more first, so we don't tell them something that isn't true."

"But they could get cheated if they sell their homes without knowing about it."

"And if they don't sell because of what we tell them and the project doesn't happen - then who do you think they'll blame?"

"Oh, yeah." Karen was silent for a moment, twisting the end of her braid impatiently. "But we've got to do something."

"You're right. Why don't you talk to some more of the kids on the street and see if any of their parents are talking to this Bellamy character."

"Okay," Karen said slowly. "But it seems like such a big secret. I don't know if they'll talk about it."

"Davey did."

"Well, yes ... but I kind of had to make up some things to get him to tell me. I didn't like that."

Mr. Gunderson sat back in his chair and didn't say anything for a long moment. He looked up at a corner of the ceiling with his unfocused eyes and a soft sad smile on his lips. "Good for you, Karen. I told you you kids know a lot. The people I used to work with – and me, too – we all told those kind of stories without a second thought. I'm sure that's what Mr. Bellamy is doing."

"Mr. Wilson, too," Karen said bitterly.

Mr. Gunderson frowned. "Mr. Wilson? You mean Joe Wilson down at the bank?"

"Yes, him."

"What kind of stories is he telling?"

"He's telling people their houses aren't worth anything, and that Davey's parents took their house off the market because nobody wanted it. But that's not true, and he knows it. He set up the deal for Davey's house with Mr. Bellamy." She said it in a burst of anger, but immediately tried to control herself.

Fortunately Mr. Gunderson was too busy trying to figure out what it meant to ask her how she knew all that. "Joe Wilson? If they've got the bank working for them, this has to be very big. I can make a few calls to try to track down Townsend Trust and Mr. Bellamy, but it would really help if you could find out if they're making offers on any other houses in town, particularly in this neighborhood."

"Okay," Karen said reluctantly, wondering how she could do it without lying or telling any more secrets. This was getting complicated.

Chapter 8: The Kids of Pond Street

The plan Karen came up with depended on Davey Torvald. If Karen asked the kids about Mr. Bellamy, she knew they would ignore her. But with Davey's status, if he asked, they'd jump right in line.

The next morning, Karen and Davey rode the bus to school as usual, Davey in the back with his friends, Karen in the middle, with the seat where Eva used to sit empty beside her. When the bus pulled up at school, kids were clustered around the front entrance, as usual. They were running, walking, and standing around; laughing, yelling, and talking, using every last minute of freedom to the fullest before they had to go in, sit still, and be quiet. Davey got off the bus in the middle of his pack of friends. Karen had to practically push her way through them to get Davey's attention, but none of them noticed, because, to them, she was invisible. When she caught Davey's eye, she nodded toward the corner of the building and walked confidently in that direction. Davey's friends went inside, but Davey told them he'd left something on the bus and ran back. When he didn't think they could see him, he snuck around the corner to where Karen was waiting.

"What'd you find out?" he asked eagerly.

"He's the one," Karen said. "He's going around trying to pull the same trick on other people, and Mr. Wilson is helping him."

"Great." Davey's face twisted into a nasty smile. "I can't wait to tell my dad and show him that guy made a fool of him."

"I don't think you should, yet. You want your parents to get a fair price, don't you?"

"Yes, but ..."

"There's only one way to do it," Karen said with such certainty that it cut off Davey's protest. "We've got to find out who else he's trying to fool and get them all together to fight this. Then your parents can get a new deal at the right price, and that would mean a lot more money."

"Really?"

"Yeah."

"But how do we find out who he's going after now?"

Karen said, "The kids'll know. All we've got to do is ask them."

"Right," Davey said enthusiastically.

"Here's how we do it. We go after our street first. After lunch, you get all the kids from Pond Street together over by the jungle gym. Then we can tell them what's going on and ask if any of their parents are thinking about selling. The kids will listen to you."

"Oh." Davey wasn't so enthusiastic anymore. "But you'll be there, too. Right?"

"Of course."

"'Cause I don't understand all this stuff as good as you do."

"Don't worry," Karen said confidently. "You know all you need to know."

This was the weakest part of the whole plan, Karen thought. Davey wanted to help. He believed in the plan, but he was surprisingly shy. At recess, Karen held her breath while Davey went up to Matt Talbot. Matt was one of Davey's best friends. Davey said something to him and Matt looked surprised, but then he shrugged and nodded his head. That's one, Karen thought.

By Karen's count, there were twelve kids that Davey had to ask – thirteen if you counted the Carlson twins as two. Matt was a seventh grader, like Davey. The other seventh grader was Jenny Stumpf. She had red hair and freckles, and she was a little chubby – not part of the in crowd. When Davey asked her, she was so shocked that he was talking to her, all she could do was nod and giggle. She'd be there.

Davey worked down through the sixth grade – Alex Cotter and Meg Carol– then three kids in fifth and two more in fourth. He looked awkward asking the third graders, but every one he asked nodded "yes." Most of them acted like they had just met a movie star. Karen thought that was silly, but she was happy with the results.

When Davey finished with the third graders, the only ones left were the Carlson twins, who were playing on the jungle gym. Instead of going up to them, though, Davey came over to stand near Karen. He took a deep breath and his shoulders slumped as he let it out. "That was hard," he said without looking at her.

"You did great," Karen said warmly.

She saw a smile twitch at the corners of his mouth and his shoulders rose again. "You think so?"

"I couldn't have done it."

"I guess not," Davey agreed.

"Are you going to ask the Carlsons?"

"Aww, they're just first graders. They're not going to know anything."

"You never know. We should ask them."

"Well then, you do it."

"Okay."

Karen felt that Davey had already risked his reputation enough talking to kids like Jenny Stumpf and the third graders.

She moved over to the jungle gym, where one of the twins was hanging upside down from the top bar. Her sister was standing on the ground beneath her, pretending she was going to catch her when she fell, and giggling her head off. They were two skinny little girls with wispy white-blond hair and missing front teeth. One was named Jenny, the other Penny, but Karen could never tell which was which. She didn't think their teacher could tell either, and she wondered if their mother could.

"Hey Jenny," she said.

Both twins looked blankly at her, shocked that one of the big kids would talk to them.

"Hi Penny," Karen went on. "You guys live on Pond Street, right?"

"Yeah," said the one hanging upside down.

"Well, we're having a meeting of all the kids from Pond Street at lunchtime. It's pretty important. Davey Torvald set it up. All the kids are going to be there. Can you come? We're going to meet right here."

"Davey Torvald?" said the one on the ground, and started to giggle again.

The other flung herself off the bar and landed on her side in the soft sand of the playground. There was a solid thump when she hit the ground, but it didn't seem to bother her. She looked up at Karen and said. "We'll come."

"Good. I knew we could count on you. See you at lunch."

Karen thought the lunchtime meeting of the Pond Street kids was the weirdest thing she had ever seen at school. Fifteen kids stood around in a circle, looking at each other and wondering what in the world was going on. They all knew each other from growing up on Pond Street, but the differences in age meant that they were almost strangers at school. Again, Karen had to admit that Davey Torvald was the only one that could have called them all together. She pushed him out front to start the meeting.

"Um, hi," Davey said uncomfortably, staring at the ground in front of him while his face turned red. "There's something going on that, um ..." He looked over at Karen with panic in his eyes.

She realized immediately that Davey wasn't going to be any good at explaining the situation and what they wanted. She stepped up beside him and looked out at the ring of puzzled faces. "Davey asked you to come to this meeting," she began smoothly in a clear strong voice, "because there's something happening on Pond Street that could affect all of us."

Suddenly all the faces focused on her. Karen felt a shiver of excitement running up her back. She was surprised how good it felt. "There's a man going around, trying to buy up some of the houses on our street, and he's fooling some people into selling them for a cheap price. We need to get together and stop him before he cheats everybody on the street and we all have to move away."

"Hey Davey," Matt called out, "is that the guy who bought your house?"

Davey looked stricken. "Um, yeah," he mumbled.

Jenny Stumpf said, "My parents talked to somebody like that. My dad said we'd have to sell if he loses his job at the factory."

The lunchtime meeting of the kids of Pond Street was
the weirdest thing she had ever seen

Suddenly all the kids wanted to tell their stories, and it went right down the line according to age – sixth graders, then fifth, then fourth. Karen had a piece of paper and a pencil. She quickly noted each kid that said their parents were thinking about selling, and whether they had talked to anybody who sounded like Mr. Bellamy. When they got through the third grade, Karen had six houses on her list.

She looked at the twins, who were sitting cross-legged on the grass, watching with wide eyes. "What about you guys?" she asked gently. "Have you heard anything about selling your house?"

One of them started nodding. "Uh-huh," she said around a finger that was stuck in the side of her mouth.

"What?"

Her sister started crying. "I don't want to move away. I like our room."

The first one took her finger out of her mouth. "Mommy said we have to go to bed early tonight, because a man is coming to talk about buying our house."

"He's coming to your house tonight?"

"Uh-huh."

Chapter 9: Mr. Bellamy

That afternoon, when Karen read Mr. Gunderson the list of houses she got from the kids of Pond Street, she felt funny about leaving out her own house, but her mother had specifically told her not to discuss their problems with Mr. Gunderson. She was relieved that it didn't seem to matter. Mr. Gunderson was excited about all the families that were thinking of selling, but he wasn't ready to do anything about it. Karen was disappointed, but she didn't say anything. She had a crazy idea, and she didn't want him to stop her.

Karen's mother worked late that night, so Karen didn't have to explain why she left the house to walk up the street to the Carlsons'. It was just before eight o'clock, the time Mr. Bellamy was supposed to show up to talk to Mr. and Mrs. Carlson about selling their home. The sun was down, but twilight still made it through the trees onto Pond Street. In the woods, the crickets were making their familiar music. The porch light was on at the Carlsons' house, but she couldn't see anyone looking out the windows, so she went up the walk and sat down on the front steps.

Of course, Mr. Bellamy was nothing like the monster she had imagined. He drove up in a fancy new car, big and black. He parked right in front of the Carlson's house and came up the walk toward Karen with a smile on his face. He was tall and slightly pudgy, with a soft fat face and thin brown hair. He wore a dark suit with a red tie and polished black shoes.

"Hello," he said in a hearty, friendly way. "You must be one of the Carlsons' little girls."

"No," Karen said without any friendliness at all, "I'm not. Who are you?"

"My name is Jerry," he said, some puzzlement creeping into his smile.

"Jerry Bellamy?" Karen asked. She continued to sit in the middle of the Carlson's front steps, blocking the man's way to the door.

"Yes. How did you know?"

"You've been talking to a lot of people on this street."

"Not really," he said. "Do you live here?"

"It's my street. What are you doing here?"

Now Mr. Bellamy looked very surprised and confused. "I have an appointment with Mr. and Mrs. Carlson. Do you ... Is there a problem?"

Karen jumped up. "You're trying to trick them," she accused in a loud and angry voice. "You want to buy their house because you know it's going to be worth more. That's not fair."

Behind her, she heard the front door open. "What? Karen?" Mr. Carlson sounded surprised and confused.

Karen hopped off the steps and ran past Mr. Bellamy, turning at the end of the walk. "Don't listen to him, Mr. Carlson. He's trying to trick us," she yelled before she ran down the street, back to her house.

When she got home, Karen put on her pajamas and sat at her desk. Her hands were still trembling with excitement as she began to write:

> You won't believe what I just did. I yelled at a man who's trying to buy up houses on Pond Street. He's part of some big project that will make the houses worth a lot when it's finished. If he buys them now, his company makes all the money and the people who

owned them don't get any of it. It made me so mad I yelled at him to go away and stop trying to cheat us. Can you imagine – me yelling at a grownup man? I was so scared I didn't even know what I was saying, but you should have seen his face. That made it all worthwhile. Do you think I'm a brat?

The problem is, I don't think it did any good, anyway. That man isn't going to be scared away by some bratty little girl. I'll probably just get in trouble for it. Oh well.

Karen was in bed when her mother got home, but she wasn't sleeping. She got out of bed and went into the front room, where her mother was sitting at the table looking at an advertising flyer. Mrs. Taylor looked up and smiled the sweet soft smile that was only for Karen. Karen pulled out a chair and sat across from her mother.

"Mom," she asked seriously, "how much money is our house worth?"

"Funny, that's just what I was wondering." Mrs. Taylor sighed. "I guess the only way to find out is to sell it."

"But what if somebody bought it for less than it's worth?"

"Well, that shouldn't happen. If everybody gets a chance to buy it, and you sell it to the person that's willing to pay the most for it, then that's what it's worth. That's how the real estate market is supposed to work."

"Does it always work?" Karen asked.

"I don't know. It doesn't really work very well if there's no one that wants to buy."

"What if there's just one person?"

"Then that person gets to decide what it's worth."

"But what if the other person doesn't want to sell for that price?"

"Then I guess nobody knows what it's worth."

"Well the person who doesn't want to sell knows what it's worth to them."

"Yes." Karen's mother smiled sadly and looked past Karen into the distance. "Yes, they do, but maybe not in dollars and cents."

Chapter 10: In the Swamp

The next day at school was a mess. When she got on the bus in the morning, she had to walk up the center aisle past Davey Torvald. He looked up at her for just a second, but the look in his eye startled her. It was a dark look of anger and hurt, but there was also something desperately pleading about it. On top of the embarrassment and anxiety she was feeling about her foolish confrontation with Mr. Bellamy the night before, that look haunted her all day. At one point, the teacher called on her to answer a question, and Karen had to admit that she hadn't heard what the teacher asked. In fact, she had no idea what the teacher had been talking about. That was something that never happened to Karen.

Then, as she was walking out to the bus after school, she saw Davey standing in the alcove by the big double doors to the gym. His eyes still held a somber hint of the look she'd seen that morning. When he caught her eye, he nodded his head toward the doors and went into the gym. Karen followed as he led her around the bleachers to where they had talked before.

He turned to her and the dark look shot from his eyes. "We've got to do something," he whispered urgently. "My dad's all messed up. He's fighting with my mom and … and … it's horrible. What can we do?"

"I don't know," Karen said helplessly. "Why is he all messed up?"

"Money." Davey said it like it was a dirty word. "He's not making enough to pay the bills anymore, and he's scared he's going to get fired. My mom says we should have got more for the house, and they're yelling and screaming at each other. I can't take it."

"But there's nothing we can do. They already signed the papers, right?"

"Yeah, but that guy fooled them. And Mr. Wilson, too. Isn't there something we can do?" Now there was nothing but pleading in Davey's eyes.

"I don't think they broke the law," she said, shaking her head sadly. Suddenly she wanted to help him more than anything. "I think the only thing we can do is keep trying to figure out what they're up to and use it to try to get your parents a better deal. But we still don't know anything, really. Telling your father he got fooled would just make things worse."

"Yeah, I guess." Davey slumped hopelessly against the bleachers. "It's just … we've got to do something."

"Don't worry. We'll figure something out," Karen said, but it still felt like she was lying to him, and that felt worse than ever.

They had to run to catch the bus, and when they did, they went to their separate seats as usual. They didn't say anything or look at each other when they got off in front of the McAllen's house. Karen went straight to the Gunderson's. There was so much on her mind. She couldn't wait to talk it over with Mr. Gunderson.

Mrs. Gunderson answered the door smiling. "Not today, dear. Mr. Gunderson is making some calls to his old friends from work. He seems quite excited about this little plot you've uncovered. It's wonderful to see him like this."

She gave Karen a dollar and asked her to come again the next day. "I know he'll have a lot to talk to you about."

Karen crossed the weedy strip between her house and the Gunderson's feeling very sorry for herself. She felt responsible for Davey's awful situation, and she couldn't talk things over with Mr. Gunderson. And, as soon as her mother got home, Karen knew she would push her to go out and find some kids to "play" with.

But her mother wasn't home yet, and Karen knew what made her feel better when she got like this. She rushed into her room and changed out of her school clothes into her jeans and hiking boots in seconds. Then she was out the door and onto the path, heading out for a tromp in the woods.

Her feet were just finding their old familiar tromping rhythm, when she happened to look down in the swamp, where she saw a woman in rubber boots and long pants moving very slowly along the edge of a small pond. A camera dangled from her neck, and a stray shaft of sunlight reflected off the lens. A little deeper in the swamp, another figure, a man, stood with his back to her. He seemed to be looking very intently into another small pond. He too, had a camera. It wasn't until he turned slightly that Karen realized he was Ron, the young man she'd seen in the woods making a map for the project. He suddenly stopped and stood motionless, apparently watching one spot in the water. After standing there frozen for more than a minute, he raised the camera to his eye and peered through it at the same spot, again completely still.

Karen couldn't figure out what he was doing. He was only thirty yards away. She could have called to him, but he seemed so intent and silent, she didn't want to break the spell. Instead, she picked her way down the slope into the swamp.

He didn't notice her until she was only 10 feet from where he stood. He nodded slightly and slowly put a finger to his lips, signaling her to be quiet. She stopped and stood still right where she was, while he put the camera to his eye again and waited. After a few minutes, Karen was getting restless. Finally, she heard the camera faintly click several times in quick succession. The man let the camera dangle and moved over to where Karen stood.

"Come on," he whispered, and he led her over to the woman, who was still moving stealthily along the bank of another pond, her eyes searching the water.

"I think I got one," Ron said to her. "Let's go take a look."

The woman finally looked up. She was tall and thin, with a long narrow face and a sharp pointed nose. "Did you get the markings?"

"I think so."

"Great," she said, then looked at Karen and smiled. "Who's this?"

"This is Karen," Ron said. "Karen, meet Janice. Janice is helping me track down our elusive little friend here."

Karen didn't know what he was talking about, but she shook hands with the woman, who seemed nice. They all climbed up the bank and sat on a large flat rock. Ron fiddled with his camera for a moment and a big excited smile lit up his face.

"Got it," he said, and he handed the camera to Janice.

She looked at the back of the camera for a moment. "Beautiful," she breathed. She handed the camera to Karen.

On the little screen on the back of the camera, there was a picture of a lizard swimming to the surface of the water. The lizard had a small blunt head, a long tail, and pink and yellow spots on the upper side of its skinny body. Karen thought it was cute.

"You think that shows enough to send out?" Ron asked Janice.

"For comment? That's plenty," she said. "You can see the toes, front and back, the markings, the shape of the head, the tail, the eyes. We'll get a flood of mail. They've never seen this one before."

"Janice is our resident amphibian specialist," Ron explained to Karen. "After you told me about this swamp the other day, I came back to check it out. That's when I saw this little guy. The first thing I did when I got back to school was tell her about him."

Janice laughed. "And I didn't believe him. You don't find a new species of salamander every day, especially not in your own back yard."

"You really think it's a new species?" Ron asked eagerly.

"From what I see – yes," Janice said. "But we'll need a lot more data to prove it."

"Are you a scientist?" Karen asked Janice.

"No," she laughed. "We're grad students. If we grow up to write good papers and teach in good colleges, we might be considered scientists someday. Right now, we're just students, but if I'm right, this funny-looking little salamander is going to help us get there. He's an amazing find."

"I thought you were a surveyor," Karen said to Ron.

"I'm that too, but only part time. Even grad students have to eat."

"So, you mean you came out here just to look for … that?" Karen pointed at the camera.

"That's exactly what we came for. But a new species? That's way more than we could have hoped to find."

"You mean nobody's ever seen one of these before?"

"Well, Janice is the expert, and she doesn't think so, but now we've got to prove it."

"Why?"

Janice laughed. "That's too hard a question for a scientist – or even a grad student."

Ron smiled, and Karen guessed that it was some kind of joke for adults. She smiled politely, too, even though she didn't get it.

"I guess," Ron explained, "the idea is to find out as much as possible about every living thing on earth. Then maybe someday somebody who is very smart – much smarter than me – can put it all together and understand how it all came to be, and how it all fits together to form life on this planet."

"But how come nobody's ever seen one before?"

"Probably because nobody's ever looked. Did you ever see any other biologists walking around in that swamp?"

"I never see anybody out here."

"Well, there you go."

"You mean this is the only place they live?"

"Could be," Janice said seriously. "But there's only one way to find out. You want to help us catch one?"

They had some equipment nearby. Janice and Ron and Karen got the equipment and spent the next hour trying to catch one of the spotted salamanders. It was fun, but they couldn't talk much and they had to move slowly and carefully, because the salamanders were very shy. They stayed about 20 feet apart, circling around on opposite sides of the small ponds. Janice told Karen to raise her hand and stay perfectly still if she saw one. Janice or Ron – whoever was nearer - would bring a net and try to capture it. Then they'd take it back to school in a small case they had prepared with a thick bed of damp moss.

They found lots of frogs, turtles, tadpoles, even a snake, but none of the rare salamanders. Karen was watching the time. She hadn't done her homework or the breakfast dishes and she wanted to help her mother fix dinner. She was about ready to tell Ron she had to go home, when he suddenly went very still and put his hand up. She stopped and stayed perfectly still, barely breathing, while he slowly reached out his net and suddenly brought it down on a spot near the edge of the pond.

"I got him. I got him," he yelled.

Karen ran over to him as he twisted the net and lifted it out of the water. In the bottom of the net, Karen could see a clump of mud and weeds, with something frantically wriggling in it. Ron held the net carefully closed, so that the wriggling creature could not get out.

"Karen, would you open that case. I've got to get him in there, which could be tricky. And one other thing. Whatever happens, don't touch this guy. Sometimes they have poisons on their skin that could make you sick."

Janice came up to them just as Karen opened the case and Ron made the transfer. He let the whole mess of mud and weeds fall into the case with the salamander, then snapped the lid down and breathed a sigh of relief. Together, the three of them watched through the clear plastic sides of the case until a small head poked out of the clump and looked around. The eyes looked like little black beads to Karen, and it was hard to say exactly what they were looking at. The head moved so quickly from one side to the other that she could hardly see it move. It would just suddenly be in a different position than it had been in the instant before. Then it would be motionless for some time before it suddenly shifted again. At one point, Karen moved slightly, and the head turned abruptly toward her, apparently studying her just as she was studying him. Karen wondered what she looked like to the tiny animal.

They watched the salamander for several minutes until it finally became bold enough to pull itself out of the weeds and moss. Janice and Ron said nothing, but Karen could sense their excitement when they saw the yellow and pink spots on its back. With its sudden, jerky movements, the salamander advanced to the wall of the little case, seeming to nudge the plastic with its head.

"He's the one," Janice said. "I can't wait to get him into the lab."

"What do you mean?" Karen asked, alarmed. "You're not going to hurt him, are you?"

"Not at all," Ron quickly assured her. "He's going to be treated like a prince. All we've got to do is get a tiny tissue sample for genetic analysis. Otherwise, we won't touch him. He'll have the best food and care that we can give him. In a couple days, we'll be bringing him back out here to let him go, right where we found him."

"You promise?"

Janice said, "You can come out and help us release him, if you want."

"Really?"

"Why not. You helped catch him."

"That'd be great. I want to be sure he's okay, you know. He's really cute."

Chapter 11: Mr. Bellamy's Tricks

When Karen got home, she was a muddy mess, but the search for the little spotted salamanders had done what her tromp in the woods was supposed to do. It had pushed aside all the frustrations of a difficult day. Karen had almost forgotten about Davey and house prices and projects in the woods.

Normally, she would have been eager to tell her mother about the salamanders, but now, she thought it would probably lead to another lecture about why she should have been playing with the kids in the neighborhood, rather than helping a bunch of adults catch salamanders. Karen didn't need that. She hoped she could sneak in and get cleaned up before her mother noticed her muddy clothes and started asking questions.

As she took off her boots on the front step, she realized her chances weren't very good. She could hear the steady whine of the vacuum cleaner coming from inside. When she was cleaning, her mother always noticed the dirt that Karen brought into the house. Karen shrugged and went in anyway, ready to face the lecture.

Her mother was bent over, vacuuming under the coffee table. When she saw Karen, she shut off the vacuum and said, "Karen, where have you been. You're all dirty." But she didn't wait for a reply before rushing on. "Run and get cleaned up. You need to get your homework done early. We've got company coming tonight."

"Huh?" Karen had been so focused on avoiding the lecture, she wasn't prepared for her mother to just skip it.

"That man who might be interested in buying our house is coming over to take a look. He's going to be here at 8:00, so you need to get your homework done first."

"He's coming here?" Karen said in shock.

"Yes. Eight o'clock. Have you got wax in your ears? Now get moving."

"Okay. I, uh ... I just remembered I forgot one of my books over at the Gundersons'. I've got to run over and get it. I'll be right back."

Mrs. Gunderson answered the door. "Yes, Karen?" she asked, a little alarmed at Karen's muddy appearance and obvious distress.

"Hello Mrs. Gunderson," Karen blurted. "I need to talk to Mr. Gunderson. It's ... it's an emergency."

"Oh my. Come in." Mrs. Gunderson held the door as Karen burst into the room. "It's Karen, Hal. She needs to talk with you urgently."

Mr. Gunderson was sitting in his chair, with an old-fashioned table radio chattering out the news. He turned it off. "What is it, Karen?"

"Mr. Bellamy. He's coming here. To my house. Tonight," she said, all out of breath.

"He is?"

"Yes. He wants to talk to my mom about buying our house. What do we do?"

Mr. Gunderson thought for a few seconds. "This could be our chance. He'll put pressure on your mother to sell, and we can catch him in the act. What time is he coming?"

"Eight o'clock."

"Good. Let's give him some time to make his pitch. I'll get Mrs. Gunderson to bring me over about 8:30."

"Shouldn't we warn my mom?" Karen asked.

"I don't think so. She might get angry and give it away. We want Mr. Bellamy to pull all the tricks he can think of. Then we can tell everybody what to watch out for. But – and this is the hardest part – you've got to make him think you don't know about the project. Can you do that?"

"Yeah, I guess so, but ..."

"What?"

"Well, he already knows me, and he knows I'm not on his side."

"What do you mean?"

"Last night I ... I just got so mad, I couldn't help it. I knew he was going to talk to the Carlsons, so I went there and yelled at him to go away and stop trying to trick people into selling their homes. I guess that was dumb, huh?"

Mr. Gunderson's mouth dropped open and he stared past Karen. Suddenly he burst out laughing. Karen didn't quite understand the joke, but she was relieved that he wasn't mad at her.

"Oh, I wish I could have seen that," Mr. Gunderson said. "I bet he's never had that happen before."

"You mean I didn't spoil everything?" Karen asked hopefully.

"I don't think so. We're going to confront him tonight anyway, right?"

"Yeah, but he's going to be pretty mad at me."

"Maybe, but he won't show it. Believe me, he's going to try to be your best friend."

"Hah," Karen snorted bitterly.

"Right, but don't worry. I'll be there before he leaves, and we'll fix him. One of my old friends told me the firm he works for, and I know some of the people there."

"Good."

"Remember, don't let him know how much you know. I'll ring your doorbell about 8:30, but I'll have Mrs. Gunderson watching out the window. If he starts to leave, we'll come right over."

"Okay," Karen said eagerly. "We've got him now, don't we?"

Mr. Gunderson smiled, his sightless eyes pointed off into the distance. "I think we do, Karen," he said. "I think we do."

While she did her homework, Karen watched her mother clean until they could have eaten off the floor. They didn't, of course, but dinner was so rushed, Karen wasn't sure what they ate. When Karen had the last bite on her fork, Mrs. Taylor whisked the plates away. She quickly washed all the dishes and put them away in the cupboard. Then she looked around their little house, which was now as neat and clean as Karen had ever seen it. She was just about to sit down when the doorbell rang.

Karen sat on the couch while her mother went to the door. She felt foolish and angry sitting there in her good dress, with her hands folded in her lap, waiting to smile and play the good little girl for a man who had come to cheat her mother. It was only by reminding herself of the surprise that was in store for Mr. Bellamy that Karen managed to keep the silly smile on her face as her mother brought Mr. Bellamy into the room and introduced him.

Mr. Bellamy put down his briefcase and held out a hand, like a peace offering. His face seemed to suppress a nasty grin. "Hello, Karen," he said. "I believe we've already met."

"Hello, Mr. Bellamy," Karen said, putting her hand in his and watching her mother's face turn puzzled.

"You've already met?" she said.

"Yes," Mr. Bellamy laughed. "Karen ambushed me last night when I went to talk to one of your neighbors. I'm afraid she doesn't approve of my business here."

Her mother turned to Karen with a look of blank surprise. "You didn't tell me about that, Karen."

"I'm sorry, Mom," Karen said, feeling a stab of guilt as she told the story she had already made up. "I heard about Mr. Bellamy from one of the Carlson twins and I was so upset that he might buy their house and make them move away that I went over and said some things I shouldn't have said. I'm sorry, Mr. Bellamy. I know it was none of my business, and it was a very childish thing to do."

"It certainly was, Karen," her mother said with a stern frown. "We'll talk about this later. I just hope you can control yourself and behave properly now."

"Yes, Mom." Karen had to swallow her anger and embarrassment, but she was furious with Mr. Bellamy. Here he was going around the neighborhood trying to cheat everyone out of their homes, and she was the one who had to apologize to him. She had to clamp her mouth shut and remember that she and Mr. Gunderson would soon make him sorry he ever set foot on Pond Street.

She followed along while her mother showed Mr. Bellamy around the house. There wasn't much to see. Karen's room was neat but crowded with the single bed, the tiny bureau, and her writing desk. Her mother's room was slightly larger, with a double bed, a bigger bureau, a mirror and a little dressing table and chair. The bathroom was a bathroom, with a tub, a sink, a toilet, and just enough room to swing the door open. Then there was the front room, with the kitchen, the table, and the living room all in one. Mr. Bellamy smiled and said everything looked very nice and well-kept, but Karen didn't think he was really very interested.

They went out and walked around the house in the twilight. Mrs. Taylor pointed out the garden and how far their property extended into the woods. Mr. Bellamy seemed more interested in this, and he asked if the ground got soggy when there were heavy rains.

"Oh, no," Mrs. Taylor said. "It all drains into the swamp back there." She pointed off through the trees to a patch of brush that was only visible as a deeper shade of darkness.

"How far is it out to the swamp from here?" Mr. Bellamy asked.

"Oh, it's a good forty or fifty yards, I'd say."

"That's good. You never want to be right on top of a swamp, do you? I mean the bugs and all."

"That's right," Mrs. Taylor agreed. "I can't say we don't get our share of bugs, but not any worse than any of the other places on the street."

As if to demonstrate what she meant, the mosquitoes suddenly found them. An irritating buzz seemed to surround them and they began slapping and scratching. They quickly retreated into the house.

Karen and her mother sat on the couch, while Mr. Bellamy took the easy chair. He opened his briefcase and pulled out a folder. Mrs. Taylor leaned forward and fussed with the mat that covered a stain on the coffee table. Karen looked up at the clock, which said 8:15.

"Before we get down to particulars," Mr. Bellamy started off grandly, "I want you to understand the nature of my business...." And he gave a long and boring speech about his company and their "mission." He made it sound like the only thing they cared about was helping families in distress. As her mother listened politely, Karen just got madder and madder. She knew that most of what he was saying wasn't true, and of course, he never said anything about the project out in the woods. When he finally got around to naming the price he was willing to pay for their house, he acted like he was doing them a favor.

"But that barely covers the mortgage," Mrs. Taylor groaned. "There'd be nothing left for us."

Mr. Bellamy shook his head sadly, but Karen saw the hint of a nasty grin on his face as he cast a brief sideways glance at her. "I'm sorry," he said, "but that's probably more than it's worth. And, as I'm sure you know, the bank is quite concerned about your ability to pay off the mortgage. If you were to turn down this offer, they would have to foreclose immediately. None of us want that. It would ruin your credit forever."

"But where would we go?" Karen's mom shook her head helplessly, tears welling in her eyes.

"I'm sure we could allow you some time to work that out."

"Really?" Karen's mom tried to discretely wipe the tears from her eyes.

When Karen saw that, her anger toward Mr. Bellamy rose up like a sudden storm. As she watched him flip through the papers in his folder her eyes narrowed and her teeth ground together hard, bulging out the muscles in her jaw. For a moment she wore the face of an angry demon. Fortunately, Mrs. Taylor and Mr. Bellamy were so intent on the contents of the folder, neither of them noticed.

Mr. Bellamy pulled two sheets of paper from the folder and slid them across to Karen's mother. "If you sign this agreement, I'll go to the bank in the morning and clear it with them. Then you'll have the $750 deposit, and you can stay in the house – as long as you keep up with your normal mortgage and tax payments - until closing. How does that sound?"

Mrs. Taylor picked up the two pieces of paper and looked at them blankly, as if they were written in a foreign language. "Okay," she said slowly.

Karen couldn't stand it. She jumped up off the couch, scowling fiercely at Mr. Bellamy. "Don't do it, Mom. He's trying to cheat us. He knows our house will be worth a lot more when his project out in the woods gets built."

Mr. Bellamy's mouth dropped open, but nothing came out.

"Karen!" her mother said, shocked. "What …"

Just then, the doorbell rang.

Chapter 12: Showdown

"I'll get it," Karen called as she ran to the door.

Mr. and Mrs. Gunderson stood on the front step. Behind them, stars began to show in the purple twilight that hung over the ridge. Mr. Gunderson looked eager, while his wife seemed a little uncertain.

"Hello, Karen," Mrs. Gunderson said.

"Hello, Mrs. Gunderson."

"Is this the right time?" Mr. Gunderson whispered.

"I hope so," Karen whispered back, still a little dazed from her outburst at Mr. Bellamy.

"Well then, I'll be off," Mrs. Gunderson said, turning to walk back across the yard.

"Come on," Karen whispered, taking Mr. Gunderson's hand.

Karen's mother looked up. "Hal?" she said, confused.

Mr. Bellamy looked at the new guest and tried on an uncertain smile that he soon realized was wasted on Mr. Gunderson.

Mr. Gunderson said, "Hello Elaine. I'm sorry to barge in like this, but I thought you might need some help about now."

"I ... I don't know ..." Mrs. Taylor looked down helplessly at the form in her hands.

"Don't sign it, Mom," Karen said again, calmer this time. "Don't sign anything until you've talked to Mr. Gunderson."

Her mother looked at her in shock. "Karen, what do you know about all this?"

"Karen knows quite a bit," Mr. Gunderson answered. "In fact, she's the one who discovered Mr. Bellamy's secret project."

"There is no secret project," Mr. Bellamy snapped, glaring at Mr. Gunderson and Karen.

Mr. Gunderson smiled calmly. "Then why are you here? Why is Torville Rossi trying to buy up Pond Street?"

"Torville ..." Mr. Bellamy was stunned. "It's ... I'm ... I'm working for Townsend Investment Trust," he mumbled, sinking back in his chair. The anger drained from his pudgy face, leaving it pale and sagging.

Mrs. Taylor looked at the forms, then looked up at Mr. Bellamy. "Karen, would you fetch a chair for Mr. Gunderson. I think I would like to understand this better."

"We need to cut this off right here," Mr. Bellamy said somewhat desperately. "You don't know what you're getting into."

"Don't worry," Mr. Gunderson said. "We're not trying to kill your project. But we can't let you buy up this street for peanuts. Before anyone sells to you, they need to understand what their house could be worth when that project goes through."

"That might kill it right there," Mr. Bellamy said, standing up. His puffy face was set in an angry frown. "There's a lot of people depending on this thing. They're not going to be too happy with you threatening to kill it."

Mr. Gunderson held out the form. "Don't you want this?"

Mr. Bellamy picked up his briefcase. "You keep it, Mrs. Taylor. When they take your house away, it will remind you that I gave you a chance to sell until this guy stuck his nose in it." He turned and walked out the door.

Nobody said anything for a minute after Mr. Bellamy slammed the door behind him. Finally, Karen said, "You did the right thing, Mom. Mr. Bellamy was trying to cheat us."

"I don't know," Mrs. Taylor said. "I hope you're right. We might not get another chance." She picked up the form that was lying on the coffee table. "This way, at least we would have got something."

"You mean the deposit for signing that agreement?" Mr. Gunderson asked.

"It's not much, but it's better than nothing."

"It's a bird in the hand, all right, but I'm pretty sure Mr. Bellamy will soon be back with a better offer."

"Alright," Mrs. Taylor sighed. "You know more about this than I do, but what do we do about the bank? They're going to kick us out next month."

"Who told you that?" Mr. Gunderson asked.

"Mr. Wilson."

Mr. Gunderson frowned. "I think Joe might have given you the wrong idea. If he started proceedings to take the house next month, it'd probably take him a year to get you out, and chances are he'd never take it that far, anyway. He's just putting pressure on people like us to help Mr. Bellamy buy up our homes cheap."

"Is that what his letter was all about?" Karen's mother said angrily.

Mr. Gunderson nodded soberly. "Sure looks that way to me."

Karen walked Mr. Gunderson home. When she got back, she sat with her mother at the table. Mrs. Taylor was slumped in her chair, apparently exhausted.

"Karen," she said, "how long have you been cooking this up with Mr. Gunderson?"

"I don't know," she mumbled. "A couple weeks, I guess."

"Why didn't you tell me about it?"

"I wanted to, but I thought you might not let me – you know – keep going."

"Maybe you're right. Maybe I wouldn't have. I haven't been thinking very clearly about this."

"Don't worry, Mom. Everything's working out, just like we said it would."

"I guess," Mrs. Taylor said uncertainly.

"Sure it is. When the project goes through, we can get enough money for this house to get another one."

Karen's mother was silent for a moment. When she spoke, her voice was soft and sad. "I think part of the problem is that I don't want another house. I want this one."

"I like this house, too, but we can find another one that's just as nice, especially if we get a good price for it like Mr. Gunderson was saying."

"I know, but … your father loved this house. We had such dreams for it, and for us. If we have to move away, it just seems like we're giving up on those dreams." She choked and her face clenched back tears. "… like we're giving up on him."

Karen had a hard time getting to sleep that night. Some time after her mother had gone to bed, Karen got up and turned on the lamp on her writing desk.

> Eva, this is getting weirder and weirder. That man I told you about came to our house tonight. He wanted to cheat my mother out of our house, and I had to sit there and smile like a dumb little girl. Hah! There's lots of it I don't understand, but I'm not confused about him. I

wanted to get a glass of water and throw it on him to see if he'd melt like the Wicked Witch.

Am I going crazy? I almost feel like it. My heart is pounding and my head is spinning, I'm so excited and scared. I've never done anything like this before, but I can't stop now. Mom needs my help to fight for our home. I wish you were here.

Chapter 13: The Meeting that Never Happened

When Karen got home from school the next day, she was surprised to find her mother home. She was supposed to be working at the diner that night.

"Brenda can handle it," she said. "We've got to go see the mayor."

"The mayor!"

"Yes," Mrs. Taylor frowned, "the mayor. He wants to talk to us – you, me, and Mr. Gunderson - about Mr. Bellamy. I'll tell you about it on the way."

Karen changed out of her school clothes and went next door to get Mr. Gunderson. The three of them got into Karen's mom's old car and started off to town hall. Karen sat in back and listened as her mother explained.

"Mayor Larson came into the diner for lunch. When I took his order, he said Mr. Bellamy told him what happened last night. He didn't want to talk about it there, so he asked if we could come to his office this afternoon."

"Are we in trouble?" Karen asked.

Her mother glanced at Karen over her shoulder. "I ... I don't know, Honey. I couldn't tell from what he said."

"Don't worry, Karen," Mr. Gunderson assured her. "You didn't do anything wrong."

"I didn't mean to," Karen said a little uncertainly.

The Pine Springs town hall was a boxy brick building with a flat roof. There was a blacktop parking lot beside it with spaces reserved for town officials and the citizens doing business with them. Mrs. Taylor parked in the lot and the three of them got out and walked across the blacktop to enter through the double glass doors. They went down a short hallway with doors to the left and right. The floor was well-worn black and white linoleum, buffed to a dull shine. The ceiling was suspended acoustic tiles. It reminded Karen of the building where her dentist had his office. The door of the mayor's office had his name and title painted on the pebbled glass. They went in and talked to his secretary, Mrs. Pettibone, a crabby old lady in a pink dress and gray sweater who was typing on a computer. Her glasses were narrow rectangles sitting on the end of her nose. She looked up at them over the glasses and said the mayor was on a call but would be with them shortly. It seemed as if she barely paused in her typing. Without an invitation, they took seats on a hard wooden bench along the wall to wait.

Curiosity overcame the jumpy feeling in her stomach, and Karen looked around the mayor's outer office. She quickly decided it wasn't very grand. In fact, more than the dentist's, it reminded her of the principal's office at her school. Mrs. Pettibone's desk sat in the middle, like a barrier before the mayor's personal office, which Karen assumed was through the door behind her. To her right, there was a bank of head-high file cabinets. The phone on her desk looked complicated, with lots of buttons and lights.

No one said anything. The tapping of Mrs. Pettibone's keyboard was the only sound. Karen's mom looked as nervous as Karen felt, but Mr. Gunderson sat up straight, with a confident look on his face that seemed to include a faint smile. They only waited about 10 minutes, but, to Karen, it felt like hours.

Finally, the door behind Mrs. Pettibone opened and Mayor Larson stood there with a polite smile on his face.

"Hello, Mrs. Taylor, Hal, Karen," he said. "Sorry to keep you waiting. Come in."

The mayor's big desk took up one side of the room. To the other side, a small round table and chairs were positioned by the windows that looked out to the parking lot. The mayor stood behind one chair while Karen's mom guided Mr. Gunderson to one of the others. When Mrs. Taylor sat down, the mayor did too. That left Karen standing awkwardly beside her mother's chair.

"Aren't you going to sit down," her mother asked.

"At the table?"

"Of course."

Karen said, "Oh, okay," and sat next to her mother.

The mayor, Dan Larson, was average height and weight, with light blond hair, very blue eyes, and a handsome red face that almost looked like he had a sunburn. Karen thought he must be about ten years older than her mother, but very strong and fit. The muscles in his jaw stood out like ropes under his skin. She had seen him around town many times, but had never been this close to him.

"Well," he said, "I think we all know why we're here. Mr. Bellamy was very surprised to find that you knew about the project he's been working on. He's a little upset about it."

"I guess that makes us even," Mr. Gunderson laughed. "We're a little upset about him trying to cheat us out of our homes."

The mayor frowned. "Now, I don't think that's fair. He was willing to pay the going price for those homes – actually more than the market price, since there really isn't any market for them."

"That's a fraction of what they'll be worth when his project goes through."

"Maybe," the mayor argued, his face getting redder. "But if he doesn't get those properties, the project might not go through at all. Then they'd be worthless, and that would be a tragedy, not just for Pond Street, but for the whole town. This project will bring a lot of jobs to replace the ones we're losing at the factory, good jobs with good wages, benefits, training. If you kill it, this town will dry up and blow away. No one will ever forgive you – or me."

"We don't want to stop it," Mr. Gunderson said mildly. "But we don't want to be forced out of our homes to make it happen. We want to make sure our neighbors know what their homes could be worth before they sell them."

"That could hold up the whole project and cost a million dollars or more. Who knows if the project will still make sense after that."

"So, you want a few families on Pond Street to contribute a million dollars to this project. That doesn't seem fair. If it's so important to the town, why doesn't the town pay the difference?"

"The town doesn't have a million dollars for that," the mayor snapped.

"Neither do we," Mr. Gunderson replied calmly.

Karen was shocked that Mr. Gunderson would argue so boldly with the mayor, but she thought that everything he said was right. Maybe that was why he felt so comfortable saying it.

The mayor wasn't shocked. He sighed and shook his head wearily. "I was never comfortable with this part of the project. As you say, it does seem a little unfair, but we had to think about what's best for the town. This project is a matter of life or death for Pine Springs, and Jerry convinced us that buying up Pond Street was life or death for the project."

"I don't believe that," Mr. Gunderson said mildly. "What's so important about Pond Street?"

The mayor's brow bunched in a perplexed frown as he looked around the table. "How much do you know about ... all this?"

Mrs. Taylor was first to respond. "I just heard of it last night."

Karen mumbled, "Not much."

"We know it involves some sort of development out beyond the swamp. It's big, and it involves Pond Street," Mr. Gunderson stated flatly.

"Just enough to be a problem," the mayor muttered. "How did you find out?"

Karen was startled, realizing that she was the source of the mayor's problem, but Mr. Gunderson replied smoothly, "We'd rather not say. Let's just say we put two and two together."

When Karen looked back at the mayor, he was staring right at her, with a thoughtful, questioning look. "If I tell you more, you need to promise to work with me on this. We can't let rumors go flying all over town. There are good reasons for some of this secrecy."

"We understand that," Mr. Gunderson said, "but we can't allow Mr. Bellamy to buy up any more houses on Pond Street without telling our neighbors why he wants them."

"Alright, alright." The mayor's red face flashed a look of irritation. "We'll figure that out somehow, but it can't go any farther than that. If it gets out to the rest of the town, that would be the end of it."

"So it's just Pond Street, he wants?" Mrs. Taylor asked.

"Right," the mayor nodded emphatically.

"So," Mr. Gunderson said, "we're back to my question: why? Why Pond Street?"

The mayor leaned forward. "It turns out that your street is critical for access to the new plant they want to build out there. The site is perfect, but there'll be a lot of truck traffic to and from the plant, and the only route for that traffic is Pond Street. The plan is to demolish the houses and turn it into a four lane road – two lanes in, two lanes out – a lifeline for the plant. Every other access is blocked by swampland that's too expensive to stabilize for such heavy traffic. Without access over Pond Street, the site probably wouldn't work. That's why it's so important to get the rights to the properties along the street."

Mr. Gunderson nodded. "Now it's starting to make some sense."

"Good," the mayor said. "We're back to where we started. Let's talk about where we go from here."

Karen thought the answer was obvious. "Why don't we get all the people on Pond Street and tell them about the project? Then everybody knows what's going on and we can all decide what's fair."

There was a moment of silence around the table. They all smiled at Karen's sudden entry into the adult discussion, and she knew she had spoken out of turn when she saw the embarrassment in her mother's smile. Karen was furious with herself for blurting out such a stupid remark. But then she saw the hint of satisfaction in Mr. Gunderson's smile as he nodded in agreement, and she didn't know what to think.

"I'm afraid it's not going to be as easy as that," Mayor Larson said. "Nobody can say what those houses are worth. Some people might be happy with a little more than what their's is worth today. Others are going to want to get rich."

"I don't know about that, Dan," Mr. Gunderson said. "We might surprise you. We're all part of this town, too, even if we do live off on the other side of the freeway. We want new opportunity in Pine Springs just as much as you do. Make us an offer."

"What do I base it on?"

"Good question," Mr. Gunderson said, thinking.

Despite her firm resolution to keep her mouth shut, Karen mumbled, "What about the people?"

"What?" the mayor asked impatiently.

"What about all the people?" she repeated. "Where do we go?"

There was another moment of silence while they all looked around the table for an answer. Mr. Gunderson was the first to respond. "I think that's a very good point, Karen. We all have homes here in Pine Springs, and it looks like we might have to give them up. A good starting point for the offer should be the cost of a comparable home in Pine Springs once the project is announced."

The mayor frowned. "But those houses are in the poorest part of town. That's way more than they're worth."

"I thought you said nobody knows what they're worth," Mr. Gunderson laughed.

Mayor Larson and Mr. Gunderson talked some more about how to calculate the new offers for the Pond Street homes. Karen didn't understand much of it, and after awhile, she stopped trying, but that didn't keep her from noticing something that surprised her very much: The mayor didn't seem to have a plan. Mr. Gunderson had to lead him from one point to the next. The mayor didn't like it. He kept making objections, but he didn't know what else to do. She had assumed the mayor would be in control, that he would tell them what to do, but it didn't turn out like that. In fact, it was just the opposite.

The plan that Mr. Gunderson finally got the mayor to agree to was pretty simple. Mayor Larson would ask Mr. Bellamy to prepare an offer for each of the houses on Pond Street. The offer would be based on an estimate of what it would cost to buy a similar house in Pine Springs after the project was announced. The homeowners would all be called to a meeting, where the new development would be announced and each family would receive their offer.

"This is risky," the mayor complained. "What if somebody holds out?"

"They might have done that anyway."

"True," the mayor agreed reluctantly, "but we can't let them think we were trying to trick them – the way you said. That would just make them suspicious."

Suddenly the mayor got excited. "That's right. We've got to make it positive, the best thing that's ever happened to Pine Springs – and particularly for Pond Street. So we present the new offers as if that's always been the plan."

"What about the families Mr. Bellamy talked to?" Mr. Gunderson asked.

"Those houses were already on the market. I'll just say Jerry was worried someone else would grab them before the offers were ready."

Mr. Gunderson shrugged. "If you think that'll work."

"I'm sure of it. But you need to back me up. Nobody can know about this meeting, right?"

"That's fine by me," Mr. Gunderson said.

"Me too," Mrs. Taylor said quickly.

The mayor looked at Karen. His expression was serious, and his eyes seemed to be drilling right into her head. "Okay," she mumbled, "but ..."

"No buts, Karen," he said. "This is very important."

"Yes, but what about those houses Mr. Bellamy already bought? Do they get new offers too?"

"They're done, signed and paid for."

"That's Eva Flowers' house and Davey Torvald's house, right?" Karen asked a little more forcefully.

"Right."

"Why shouldn't they get the same deal?"

"Their houses were already on the market. Jerry made them offers and they accepted. I don't see what good it would do to open those up again."

"That's not fair."

"I ..." the mayor started to say, but then he frowned and turned to Mr. Gunderson.

"They've got to get the new deal, too," the old man laughed. "Otherwise your story falls apart."

The mayor slumped in his seat. "Jerry's going to choke on that. It's like going back to square one and giving away money at the same time."

"There's no other way," Mr. Gunderson stated flatly.

"Okay, but you three have to back me on this. If it turns into a delay on the project, we're all in trouble. Remember, this meeting never happened."

None of them said anything as they walked out to the car. Mrs. Taylor helped Mr. Gunderson into the passenger seat, while Karen got in back. But, through the side window, Karen happened to glance back at the town hall building. She was surprised to find that she could see in the windows, right into the mayor's office.

The mayor was sitting at his desk, looking down at some papers, when Mr. Bellamy came into the room. He stood in front of the mayor's desk as the mayor looked up and said something to him. Suddenly, the sour expression on Mr. Bellamy's face turned to shock and then immediately to anger. He slapped the desk and seemed to shout something at the mayor, although Karen couldn't hear it. His face got all red and puffy again, but that was all she saw before they drove away.

"That wasn't anything like what I expected," Mrs. Taylor said when they were stopped at a light on Main Street.

"We knew too much," Mr. Gunderson said. "He had no choice."

"Why not?" Karen asked. "I mean, he's the mayor, right?"

"Right. Which means he's a politician – even in this sleepy little town. He's got to worry about what people think about him. He's got to get that project through, but he can't have people thinking he's willing to let Mr. Bellamy cheat us to do it. We put him in a very tough spot."

"We had to." Karen's mom was suddenly angry. "Mr. Bellamy was going to take our house and leave us with nothing."

Chapter 14: Newton Goes Home

The next day was Saturday, and promptly at 9:00 AM, Karen parked her bike in the rack and went up the steps of the library to wait for Mrs. Blevins to open up for the day.

Mrs. Blevins was the assistant librarian, a pretty young woman who was married to Richie Blevins. Two years before Karen was born, Richie Blevins was the star quarterback who led the Pine Springs High School football team all the way to the state finals, the only time in the history of the town they ever got that far. He was the closest thing to a celebrity that Pine Springs had. When he married his high school sweetheart, the wedding was all that anyone in town talked about for weeks. Karen was only in first grade at the time, but she could still remember the pictures her mother had shown her in the local newspaper. Karen liked Mrs. Blevins. Even though she was beautiful and famous (at least in Pine Springs), it hadn't gone to her head. She was always friendly and helpful.

"Good morning, Karen," Mrs. Blevins said when she opened the door. "You're as dependable as the sun. Don't you ever want to sleep in on Saturdays?"

"Good morning, Mrs. Blevins," Karen said as she followed her over to the check-out desk. "No, I get up early so I can have breakfast with my mom before she goes to work."

"Oh. Well, I'm glad you do. It would be too quiet here without you."

She handed Karen a little black cartridge that plugged into the computer to turn it on, and Karen signed the book.

The library had three computers in a little alcove off the main room. Karen chose the one by a window that looked out to a little side yard where a dogwood tree was in full bloom. As the computer was warming up, she glanced out at the beautiful white blossoms and the high rugged ridge that rose off in the distance. She thought her little town must be one of the most beautiful places in the world, though she knew the white petals would soon be on the ground, curling and turning brown.

She shook her head and logged into her email account. There was a message from Eva:

> Hi Karen,
>
> How is everything back in Pine Springs? It's getting hot here. I wonder what it will be like when summer really starts. Anyway, I'm making a few friends, but it's not like it used to be back home. I'll probably be bored out of my mind this summer. I asked my parents if I could have a puppy, and they said they'd think about it. We've got a little yard, but the grass is already turning brown. I guess a puppy wouldn't care about that. Well, I hope you're having fun.
>
> Your friend, Eva

Karen's smile had a trace of sadness as she tried to picture Eva's clear blue eyes and sweet smile. She was disturbed that the picture was already growing a little fuzzy and unclear in her mind. How could that be? They were best friends. Karen promised herself she would never let Eva fade from her life, and she knew only one way to do it. For the next hour, she poured herself into a long email about everything that she had done and thought and felt over the past week.

She typed in all the handwritten notes she'd made at her little writing desk each night, adding more comments and some silly private jokes they used to share. The meeting with the mayor was easily the biggest thing on her mind, and she ached to write down all the questions and impressions it raised. Eva would understand in a way that her mother and Mr. Gunderson could not. But she couldn't talk about it. She had promised Mayor Larson. All she said was:

> ... I'm finding out more about that man that wanted to buy our house. I can't talk about it yet – I promised I wouldn't – but it's very big and important to the whole town. It's exciting, like a mystery, but I don't like what I'm finding out about some people. I never could understand how people could do bad things to each other, but maybe that's what you learn when you grow up. When this is all over, you and me need to have a good talk, like we used to do when we were out tromping in the woods.
>
> Your best friend forever, Karen

Karen looked up from the screen and saw with bleary eyes that quite a few people had suddenly appeared in the library. The big clock over the checkout desk said 10:30. She scrolled up to the beginning of her email and was a little surprised how much there was. She hoped that Eva would get through it all. Eva wasn't much of a reader. Karen hit the send button and shut down the computer.

When she took the little black cartridge back to the checkout desk, Mrs. Blevins laughed her warm, friendly laugh. "You sure had a lot to say, huh?"

Karen laughed too. "I guess I did."

After lunch, Karen took the path out to the edge of the swamp, near the spot where Ron and Janice had caught the spotted salamander. She got there just before the time they said they'd be back to return the salamander to his home. Since they weren't there yet, Karen climbed the steep bank and sat on the flat rock to wait.

It was a warm spring day. Up in the sky, a few puffy clouds billowed and rolled, but rarely blocked the sun. There at the base of the foothills, the virgin forest had been harvested long ago. Now there were only sparse and scraggly pine covering those hills, none of the tall stately trees that sheltered the swamp. Looking down from the sunny hillside, the deep shadows gave the swamp a mysterious quality, as if it held some ancient magic. Karen lay back on the warm rock and looked up into the sky, thinking of nothing at all for the first time in days. The breeze was so gentle and the afternoon so peaceful, she fell asleep.

She dreamed she was walking through a forest of grand old trees with her father. He was walking fast and effortlessly, floating across the forest floor with that confident smile on his handsome face, while Karen struggled over the massive roots and rocks. Normally, Karen was strong and swift in the woods, but in her dream, she could not keep up with her father. He finally turned to her and said he would have to go on ahead to make sure they were on the right path. To help Karen find the way, he would leave a trail of little pink and yellow stones behind him. Karen watched him fade into the distance and began to follow the trail. But the stones turned into spotted salamanders that scurried back into the swamp, and Karen did not know which way to go.

"Karen."

She woke with a start and looked around trying to figure out where she was.

Ron was standing ten feet away with a small pack on his back, smiling at her with his laughing eyes. Janice stood beside him with the little carrying case. "Were you waiting for us?" she asked.

"Huh?" Karen said, trying to sort out the two of them, the swamp and the warm rock from her father and the forest of her dream. "Oh, yeah. Yeah, I guess I fell asleep."

"Not a bad way to pass the time," Ron said. "Sorry we're late. Traffic was crazy coming down from the city."

"That's okay," Karen said, standing up and stretching. "What time is it?"

Ron looked at his wrist, on which there was no watch. "It's about 2:30 or 3:00, I think. Want to see our little friend go back where he belongs?"

"Yeah," Karen said eagerly. "Can I peek in the box?"

Janice put the case on the ground. "Sure, but there's not much to see," she said. "He's hiding under all that moss and stuff to keep his skin moist, but you'll see him when we let him go."

Karen looked through the clear top of the case and saw that she was right. It looked like a soggy clump of moss and leaves and twigs. "Are you sure he's in there?" she asked.

"Oh yeah," Ron said, starting down the hillside, "and he's got some story to tell when he gets back to his friends. He'll probably claim he was abducted by aliens – which is a pretty good description of us. We called him Newton."

"Newton." Karen said, tromping along behind them.

"For newt," Janice said, "which is just another name for salamander."

"Is he okay?" Karen asked.

Ron laughed. "Okay? He's just had the best salamander vacation ever. He got the best food we could find. We kept the temperature just right, gave him plenty of moist vegetation to burrow in, a pool to swim in whenever he wanted. I'm not sure he's going to want to go back to the swamp."

"Really?"

"No," he said seriously. "The truth is these guys can be very sensitive to any change in their environment. We did everything we could to make him comfortable, but you never know what can harm a wild creature when you take it out of its home. Janice thinks this species has probably lived right here in this swamp for centuries – maybe thousands of years. Most likely, this is the only place where this kind of salamander has ever lived. So you can imagine how eager he is to get back home."

"Wow," Karen said, "You mean they don't live anywhere else in the whole world?"

"Not that we know of," Janice said with a trace of pride.

They were nearing the spot where Newton had been captured the week before. Karen's feet were sinking into the mud with every step. Her boots were thick and dripping with it, but she didn't even notice. She was looking at the swamp and seeing something new – a place that had been there and hadn't changed for longer than she could imagine, a place that had its own special inhabitants who lived nowhere else in the whole world. No wonder it looked magical.

"Let's be very quiet, now," Janice whispered. "I want Newton to be as relaxed as he can be when we release him."

She put the case down right beside the tiny pond and carefully took the top off. Then she and Ron opened some little latches and folded down the sides to lie flat on the ground. Now there was just the soggy clump of vegetation sitting in the middle of the unfolded box. Newton was free, although he didn't seem to notice. Nothing happened. The clump just sat there.

They all watched, perfectly silent and still, for five minutes. Finally, the little green and brown head poked out from the side of the clump. Newton's little black eyes were open wide and he looked around with that peculiar jerky motion of his head that Karen remembered. Suddenly, he jumped from the clump and scooted like lightning toward the pond. At the very edge of the water, he stopped just as suddenly. His head swiveled to look over his pink and yellow spotted back directly at the three aliens, who had not moved a muscle. Newton stayed like that, watching them for a full minute. Karen thought he was saying thank you for bringing him home, and goodbye. Then, he turned his head with a jerk, wriggled into the pond and disappeared in the murky water.

Ron folded up the case around the clump and reattached the top. They slogged back through the mud to the edge of the swamp. He put the case on the ground and shook himself out of the backpack.

"We've got to go back and see if we can get some more pictures," Janice said, taking a camera out of the pack. "I sent around a preliminary report yesterday, and I'm going to have a thousand questions waiting for me tonight. You want to come with us?"

"I've got to get home," Karen said, but she made no move to leave.

"Well, maybe we'll see you out here again. I think we'll be spending quite a few weekends observing these little guys."

"Um, could I ask you a question?"

"Sure."

"You said salamanders are sensitive about their environment. Could it hurt them if somebody built a big factory up there?" Karen pointed up the hillside.

"Yes it could," Ron said seriously. "Factories can be very toxic to the plants and animals around them – to humans, too. If there was a factory up there and they dumped anything – even the runoff from their parking lots – if they dumped it into this swamp, it could wipe out Newton and all of his kind."

"Really?" Karen frowned with concern.

"Don't worry," Janice said confidently. "Once we prove Newton is a unique species not found anywhere else, we'll have him listed as endangered, and no one will be able to put a factory up there without the proper environmental controls."

"They could do that – I mean make it safe?"

"Sure," Ron said. "Depending on what kind of factory it is, it might not even cost very much. Mostly, they've just got to make sure the water that comes down from the mountains keeps flowing through the swamp like it always has. Nothing from the factory – no water, no chemicals, no garbage, no rocks, no dirt, no people – none of that can leak out into the swamp. It sounds like a lot, but it's not really that hard."

"So anybody that wanted to put a factory here would do it. They'd make it safe for the salamanders, right?"

Ron shook his head. "Not unless we make them. Companies don't like to spend any money if they don't have to."

"But they do have to. They'd be making them extinct."

"That's right," Janice said, "but we're not going to let them. Ron and I are writing a paper to prove that these salamanders are a distinct species that exists nowhere else. Then we'll get the swamp protected by the government."

"How long does that take?" Karen asked.

Janice looked at Ron.

"I don't know," he said, thinking. "Maybe five years."

"Five years!"

"Hey, it's a legal process," he shrugged. "The science has to be solid."

"But what if somebody wants to build before that?"

"Then we've got to come up with another way."

"Don't worry," Janice laughed. "That's not going to happen. Who'd want to build a factory out here in the middle of nowhere?"

Chapter 15: Some Kid

Sunday, Karen went to church with the McAllens from up the street. Her mother couldn't take her, because Sunday morning was one of the busiest times at the diner. Mrs. Taylor thought it was important for Karen to go, so she gratefully accepted when the McAllens volunteered several years earlier. Now it was the routine. Karen accepted it too, although she still felt a little like an intruder with the older couple. They were so pious and reserved, she still felt like she hardly knew them after all those Sunday mornings.

They always went to an early service, so Karen was home by 11:00. As usual, she changed out of her good clothes and faced a few hours of free time. Her homework was done, the garden was weeded, the house was spotless, and the dishes were washed and put away. The Gundersons were having a Sunday visit with some of their friends, so she wasn't going to read that afternoon. She flopped onto the sofa and wondered what to do until her mother got home around 3:00. She didn't have to wonder for long, because the doorbell rang, and when she answered it, Davey Torvald was standing on her front step.

He was wearing sneakers, jeans, and a red and white baseball jersey. His expression was serious and he shifted from one foot to the other, but didn't say anything.

"Hi, Davey," Karen said with a slight question in her voice.

"Uh, hi," Davey answered.

Karen waited to find out what he wanted, but he didn't say any more. "Do you want to come in?" she suggested.

"Uh, no." Davey looked over his shoulder at his bike, which was lying at the side of the road. "It's a nice day, so I ... um, I thought we could ride our bikes in town. Okay?"

Karen was completely unprepared for that. She had always seen him as just another popular boy, without anything more complicated to worry about than the style of his haircut and the brand of his sneakers. Now she sensed something else going on behind his troubled blue eyes. "Okay," she said.

Davey nodded solemnly as if he'd used up all his words. Karen went back into the house and got her helmet. She stepped out on the front step and shut the door behind her, as Davey moved stiffly out of her way. Then she went around to where her bike was parked under the little shed roof that came off the side of the house. She walked the bike across her front yard and joined Davey on the pavement. He had his helmet on and was standing next to his bike.

"Ready?" she asked.

"Uh-huh."

"Okay, let's go."

They pedaled up Pond Street to where it joined the old county road. This was the part of the ride that Karen hated. To get to town – or anywhere else from Pond Street – you had to ride on the county road for about a quarter of a mile, past the on and off ramps to the interstate, then through the narrow tunnel that went under it. The speed limit was 35 on that stretch, but it seemed like it was outside of town, so most of the traffic whizzed by at 50 or more. Fortunately, there was a wide breakdown lane for Karen and Davey to ride on and not much traffic that day.

Once they got through the tunnel, the county road became Main Street. The houses along there were some of the biggest and nicest in town, but, for the first time, Karen noticed that the paint was peeling on some of them, and some of the gutters looked like they were starting to rot. Several had "For Sale" signs stuck in the front yard, and one of them was empty, like Eva's, and the gardens were ragged with weeds. Another had been turned into a rooming house, with a sign in front that said, "Vacancy, by week or month."

They rode straight through the downtown, which was quiet. Most of the stores and businesses were closed for Sunday, but Karen knew that many of them would not reopen. They were the ones where the windows were soaped so people couldn't see the depressing emptiness inside. Others had signs that said, "Final Clearance Sale." Most of them had been that way for weeks, but Karen felt like she was seeing them for the first time. She remembered Mayor Larson saying Pine Springs might "dry up and blow away."

Just past downtown, they came to the town park. It had a ball field, a couple of tennis courts, a basketball court, and a playground. Karen had been there many times when she was younger, but not so often in the past couple years. She was surprised to see the ruts and barren patches in the ball field, the cracks in the tennis courts, the pitiful shreds of net hanging from the basketball hoops, and the weeds growing in the sand of the playground.

"Hey," Davey said, "let's stop here."

Davey leaned his bike against the rusty chain link fence and walked over to the big swing set. Karen did the same and followed along. They found two swings that had unbroken seats and started swinging. There were just a few little kids over on the climbing structure. Davey pumped harder and harder, going higher and higher with each swing.

"I can bail out at the very top," he yelled.

"Davey," Karen called out, "be careful."

"Watch," he said and let go at the very top of his arc. He was at least ten feet in the air, but his timing was wrong. He started leaning too far forward, and Karen could see that he wasn't going to land on his feet. His arms and legs swung wildly, trying to correct it, and he twisted as he came down, landing on his side with a thump.

Karen dragged her feet and stopped her swing as quickly as she could, then ran to where Davey lay on the ground. "Are you all right?" she cried.

Davey leaned on one elbow, still on his side. He looked dazed, and all he could say sounded like, "Uh … uh … uh," as he gasped for breath.

"What should I do?" Karen asked frantically. "Should I run and get help?"

"Uh-uh." Davey shook his head. "I'm … okay."

It took him a minute to get his breath back, but he finally got up and started walking around. Karen walked with him.

"I can usually do that trick," he said.

"These swings go really high."

Davey managed a weak grin. "Well, I bet that's the highest I ever bailed out, anyway."

They got back on the swings, but Davey just sat there, not swinging. Karen did the same.

"You know this stuff that's going on, with the houses and the buying and selling and everything," Davey said suddenly.

"Yeah."

"No, I mean, you know what's going on. Right?"

"Some of it, I guess."

"And it's important, too. I mean, even to our parents. Huh?"

"Yes, it is."

102

"Well, how come you get to know about it, and none of the other kids do?"

"It was an accident," Karen said slowly. "I found out by accident."

"But you'll still find out if more stuff happens. Right"

"I guess so."

Davey turned his swing sideways to face her. His expression was grim, almost pleading. "I want to be in on it, too. Okay? I won't tell anybody. I promise."

Karen frowned. "It's going to come out soon, anyway – probably this week."

"That might not be soon enough," Davey said. He looked off into the distance, his eyes bleak with anger and fear. "My dad's gotten even worse. He just sits there in his chair, watching TV and drinking beer. Or he yells at me or fights with my mom. If I could just tell him some good news, it might get him back to normal. And anyway, I could help, like when we got all the kids together to ask about their houses. I helped then, didn't I?"

"Yes, you did. You helped a lot."

"I could do more."

Karen suddenly felt the need for an ally in all this, somebody who could see it the way she did, who wouldn't think her questions were silly or weird. Writing to Eva helped, but she was so far away, and she didn't write back often enough. Davey was right here.

"I don't know if there's any more to do, but I guess I can tell you some of it if you promise you won't tell anybody – not even your parents."

"I promise," Davey said eagerly.

Karen told him everything – the surveyors, Mr. Gunderson, Mr. Bellamy, the big project and what it could mean for the town. She thought it was alright because Davey had promised to keep it secret and she didn't mention the meeting with the mayor or the new offers for the houses. Besides, Davey was just a kid. The mayor wouldn't care if another kid knew about the secret project, so long as it didn't get out to the grownups.

Davey asked lots of questions and Karen answered as truthfully and as thoughtfully as she could. Davey was amazed at what he heard and clearly impressed with the inside information that Karen understood so well and no other kid in town even suspected. They talked for over an hour before Karen noticed it was almost time for her mother to get off work. Sunday afternoon was one of the rare times they got to spend together. She said it was time to go, so the two of them rode straight home. When they got to Pond Street, Davey rode up alongside Karen and said, "See you tomorrow," before he pulled into his driveway and Karen went on down to her house at the end of the street. She saw the car in the driveway and knew that her mother was already home. She put her bike under the shed and went in the front door.

"Hi, Honey," her mother said. "Out for a ride?"

"Hi, Mom. Yeah, I went in town."

"Just by yourself?"

"No. With some kid I know in school."

"Great. Maybe you've got a new friend."

"Um, yeah, maybe," Karen said.

That night, before she went to bed, Karen did not write about the bike ride into town with Davey. Instead, by the weak light of her desk lamp, she looked into the mirror for a long time, trying to find the answer to a question that was bothering her. The girl she saw looking back at her was not pretty, like some of the girls at school. Her hair was no particular color – not blond or red or black, or even brown. It was a nothing shade of dusty tan, pulled tight into braids that looked like old rope. The brown eyes that frowned critically into their own reflection looked muddy and dull. The nose had a funny rounded tip that reminded her of a rabbit. Her mouth was too wide for her face. When she tried on a smile, it looked silly and posed.

She sighed and turned out the light, then climbed into bed. That face answered her question. Davey didn't ask her to ride bikes with him because he liked her. He could do a lot better than that. She just happened to have some information he wanted. Well, that was alright. He never said anything different, and he could still be a useful ally. It made no sense to worry about what he thought of her, but she lay awake for a long time thinking about it anyway.

Chapter 16: The Mayor's Call

The next morning, when Karen walked up to the school bus stop, Davey wasn't there. This was unusual because Davey liked to horse around with Matt Talbot, showing off for the younger kids. The bus came and Karen was getting on when she saw the Torvalds' front door open. Davey burst out, running up the street as fast as he could. Mrs. Wagner, the bus driver, didn't like to wait for anything, but she could see Davey coming and she held the door open an extra 15 seconds so he could get on.

Davey leaped up the steps and paused for a moment at the front of the bus. He was a mess, which was also unusual. His hair was sticking out all over his head, his shirt was untucked, and his untied shoelaces trailed after him. His face was all puffy and blotched, and his eyes were small and dark with fear, as he scanned the bus for a seat.

"Take a seat, Mr. Torvald," Mrs. Wagner said sternly. "You're holding us up."

Matt had saved a seat for him in the back and was gesturing for him to come and sit down, but Davey shocked everyone by stopping short and plopping down in the empty seat next to Karen. Karen was so surprised, she didn't know what to do. She couldn't look at him, and she couldn't look back at all the other kids on the bus who were staring blankly at her and Davey.

Davey leaned close to her and whispered, "We've got to do something. My dad is ... I've got to tell him. We can't wait anymore."

"Davey, what's wrong?" Karen whispered back. "What's going on?"

"My dad. He's so messed up, he might hurt my mom."

"What?" Karen looked up and all the kids were still watching them. The bus had never been this quiet. "We can't talk now. Meet me at recess."

Davey groaned, but he didn't say anything more. He tried to smooth his hair down and tied his shoelaces. He stuffed his books and papers into his book bag and stuffed his shirt-tails into his pants. He looked down the aisle with such a bleak and threatening expression that all the kids turned away and tried to look like they were minding their own business. But there wasn't any loud talk or laughter that morning, and none of the usual roughhousing. The kids spoke in whispers, and Karen knew what they were whispering about – Davey and her. Mrs. Wagner decided it had been well worthwhile to wait for Davey, since it gave her the most peaceful morning she'd had on the bus in a long time. To Karen, it seemed like the longest bus ride she'd had in her whole life.

When they were getting off, Davey whispered, "Don't forget. Recess. We've got to do something. It's an emergency."

At recess, Karen and Davey snuck around the corner of the school building, and Karen found out what Davey was talking about.

"My dad got laid off from the factory last week," Davey said miserably. He'd put some water on his hair to hold it down, but the look of fear was still in his eyes. "They didn't tell me until last night. That's what they've been fighting about. He was talking crazy, blaming my mom, blaming me. I thought he was going to hit her, but he was too drunk. I can't take this. We've got to do something."

Without realizing it, he had grabbed her arm, and he was squeezing it and shaking her to emphasize his words. "Ow," Karen said. "You're hurting me."

"Oh." Davey looked down at his hand on her arm and immediately let go. "Sorry. I, uh … What can we do?"

"Did you tell them everything will be different soon?"

"I told them, but I didn't tell them how. You made me promise. My dad wouldn't believe me anyhow. He said there'll never be a job for him here, and he's sick of banging his head against the wall."

"Can't he wait just a few days?"

"We've got to tell him something to get him calmed down."

"But would he even listen to us. We're just kids."

"Maybe he'd listen to you. You know more about it than me, and you sound smarter. Would you tell him all that stuff you told me yesterday? Please."

"But I can't talk about it. I promised. You did too."

"I don't care. This is different. This is an emergency. You got to talk to him."

"Alright," Karen agreed reluctantly, "I'll talk to him, but I don't think it'll do any good."

Davey managed a small smile. "You can do it," he said. "If anybody can do it, you can."

Karen wasn't so sure about that. When she got off the bus with Davey that afternoon, she still had no idea what she would say to Mr. Torvald. Davey took her in through the front door, and they went down the short hallway to the kitchen, where his mother and father were sitting at the kitchen table. Mr. Torvald, a tall, powerfully built man with light brown hair that had thinned out to a few wisps above his forehead, sat facing the doorway where Davey and Karen came into the room. His head was bowed forward, his chin nearly resting on his chest. Mrs. Torvald had her back to them.

"Davey, could you go out ..." she started to say, then turned and saw Karen, which seemed to bring a red flush to her cheeks. "Oh. I didn't know you had a friend with you. Hello, Karen."

"Hello, Mrs. Torvald, Mr. Torvald."

Mr. Torvald raised his head to look at them. His eyes were red and unfocused and his cheeks hung loosely around a sour sneer. It seemed to cost him a great effort to put his words together. "Get out of here, Davey. We're talking."

"Dad. I brought Karen to tell you about that stuff that's going on in the neighborhood, the stuff I told you about. It's important. Just listen."

"No," his father shouted. "I told you I didn't want to hear it. Now leave us alone."

Karen stood near the door. Her legs felt weak and rubbery. She wanted to run home, but she said softly. "It's true, Mr. Torvald. There's going to be new jobs in Pine Springs soon."

Mr. Torvald frowned fiercely at her. "What new jobs?"

"I don't know," Karen said, "but Mr. Bellamy bought your house, didn't he?"

"How did you know who bought our house?"

"Because he tried to buy our house, and the Carlsons' too."

"He did?"

"That's right, and he's trying to buy up all the houses on Pond Street. He wouldn't do that unless he knew they were going to be worth more soon."

"So what. It's not going to do me any good."

"It will, Mr. Torvald," Karen said quietly. "Just wait a few days. You'll see."

"Wait," Mr. Torvald growled in frustration. "That's all I do. You kids don't know what you're talking about. Get out of here."

"Maybe we don't," Karen said desperately, "but I bet you'd believe it if the mayor told you."

"The mayor? What's he got to do with it?"

She'd used the mayor's name. It came out by accident, and now she didn't know what to do. "He's going to have a meeting," she said, rushing blindly on. "That's where you'll get the answers."

Mr. Torvald just stared at her.

"Karen," Davey's mother scolded, "you shouldn't make up things like that."

"But it's true, Mrs. Torvald."

Mr. Torvald stood up from his chair, nearly knocking it over. His face had turned red and blotchy. "Davey," he roared, "you're going to be sorry for this. I'll ..."

The ring of the telephone interrupted him. It sat on the counter, just a few steps from the table. They all turned to look at it, but after the second ring, Mrs. Torvald got up and answered. "Hello?" she said tentatively.

"What?" Her face turned blank with amazement. "He does?"

She turned and looked at Karen with bewilderment as she handed the phone to Mr. Torvald. "It's the mayor," she said.

Mr. Torvald looked at the phone and put it to his ear as if it were some strange object he'd never seen before. "Hello?"

"Um, yeah, hello." He repeated as he glanced at Karen and walked unsteadily down the hall to the living room.

Davey looked at Karen with a smile that was twisted between hope and fear. Mrs. Torvald seemed so shocked, she just stared at Karen with her mouth half open. They all listened to Mr. Torvald talking on the phone. They couldn't hear the words, but the tone was clear. Mr. Torvald was respectful and agreeable, quite a change from the rage of a moment before.

"That was the mayor," Mr. Torvald said when he came back into the kitchen. He seemed dazed. "There's a meeting at Town Hall Thursday. It's important and secret – just for the people on Pond Street."

He sat down heavily in his chair and stared at the wall.

"Karen, how did you know?" Mrs. Torvald asked.

"I can't say," Karen said miserably. "It's part of the secret. I wasn't even supposed to say what I did."

"Oh." Mrs. Torvald looked from Karen to her husband, then back to Karen. "I think we owe you an apology." She sighed and her shoulders slumped. "And thank you for trying to help. God knows we need all the help we can get."

Chapter 17: A Liar's Threat

Between one thing and another, Karen had not read to Mr. Gunderson since Thursday. First, there was the meeting with the mayor that never happened on Friday. Then, on Saturday, the Gundersons had not been home when Karen got back from helping release Newton back into the swamp. Sunday they had guests. Now it was Monday, and she was late for work.

She ran from Davey's house to the Gunderson's, bursting with questions and impressions and ideas she needed to talk over with Mr. Gunderson. It seemed so much had happened since the last time they had talked – the mayor's strange behavior, Mr. Bellamy in the mayor's office, Davey Torvald and his father, and her worries about Newton. She was counting on Mr. Gunderson. His gentle wisdom and experience would help her sort it all out.

But Mrs. Gunderson answered the door with a tissue in her hand and her eyes red from crying. "Oh, Karen, Mr. Gunderson is so sorry to miss his reading today, but he's taken a turn, and he's just not up to it."

"Oh," Karen said blankly. She felt a cloud of loneliness drift across her sun. In that moment, she suddenly saw how much she needed his guidance and support. All this amazing business she'd been involved in would never have happened without him. But he was old and sick. He could die. How could she go on without him?

"I ... I'm sorry, too, Mrs. Gunderson," she stammered. "I ... I hope he's better tomorrow."

"I hope so too, dear." A little sob seemed to catch in her throat. She reached into the pocket of her dress and pulled out a dollar bill. "Here's your pay."

"Oh, no," Karen said. "I didn't do anything."

"Yes you did," the old lady insisted. "You showed up for work, just as you were supposed to. Mr. Gunderson said to tell you that's the way it works. If you're scheduled for work and you show up, the boss has to pay you, even if he doesn't have any work for you. It's a rule."

"It doesn't seem right."

The old lady looked at her for a moment with a sad smile and a tear formed at the corner of her eye. She wiped it away with the tissue. "Karen, I could never pay you enough for what you've done for Mr. Gunderson. Now you take this dollar, and we'll both pray that he's better tomorrow."

Karen walked slowly through the weeds to her house. Suddenly all the things that had been spinning through her head were gone. They just weren't that important anymore.

Karen had not been home for more than 10 minutes. She was still lying on the couch worrying about Mr. Gunderson, when the doorbell rang. She jumped up and raced to the door, thinking it might be Davey Torvald. After pausing for a moment to collect herself, she opened the door and found Mr. Bellamy standing on the step. He wore a suit, and his face wasn't red or puffed up with anger, but Karen was startled and a little intimidated.

"Hello, Karen," he said evenly. "Is your mother here?"

"Hello, Mr. Bellamy. No, she's at work."

"Well, that's just as well. It's you I want to talk to, anyway."

"Me?"

"That's right. You. It wasn't your mother that stuck her nose into my business, was it?"

"No."

"And it wasn't your mother that got me in trouble with my boss, was it?"

"No."

"No. It was you and that blind old man next door, wasn't it?"

"I ... we didn't want to get you in trouble. It's just ... we didn't want you to take advantage of us."

Mr. Bellamy's face began to get red. "Take advantage ... I offered to buy this house when nobody else would give you a nickel for it. How is that taking advantage?"

"You didn't tell us about the project, the new plant out in the woods. You knew, but you didn't tell us."

"Why should I?" Mr. Bellamy snapped. "So I'd have to pay more? I'd have to be an idiot to do that."

"No," Karen said, suddenly feeling her own face getting hot. "You'd have to be honest, and that's something you're not. But now we caught you, and you can't lie anymore."

Suddenly Mr. Bellamy's face turned dark red and swelled up so much, Karen thought he might pop like a balloon. He ground his teeth. "You little ... Didn't your mother ever teach you any manners? Who are you to talk back to me?"

"I'm Karen Taylor," she said in a rush of anger. "This is my home. Who are you to try to take it away?"

"I'm bringing this dusty little nothing of a town the biggest thing it's ever seen, you little brat. Don't you get in my way again or I promise you you'll regret it – you and your mother, both. That feeble old man, too."

For once, Karen was too angry for words. She glared at Mr. Bellamy until he turned his puffed up purple face away and stomped down the walk to his car. Then she stood in the doorway, watching, until the big black car spun its wheels and roared off up the street. She closed the door and stumbled back to the couch, where she collapsed in a heap, trembling from head to toe.

Karen couldn't tell her mother about Mr. Bellamy's visit, because she knew exactly what her mother would do. She would go after Mr. Bellamy like a mother bear protecting her cubs, and Karen didn't want that. She couldn't tell Mr. Gunderson, either. He was too sick. Even if he was well enough to read to, she couldn't risk his health by letting him worry about something like that. And Davey had enough problems of his own. That night, in the pool of lamplight on her writing desk, Karen wrote out another note to Eva:

> I've got myself in a terrible mess. That man actually came to the door today and threatened me. Can you believe that? A grown man threatening me? I yelled right back at him and practically called him a liar – which he is – but I was scared out of my mind. Who knows what he could do. He's got a lot of important people and money behind him. I think he could make trouble for me and my mom. And the thing that stinks is that we didn't do anything wrong. He's the one who's trying to trick everybody. It's so unfair.
>
> Remember how we used to play Secrets? We'd pretend we knew something that nobody else knew and we couldn't tell them. It was fun, but it was just a game. Now I'm seeing how grownups play it. It's not a game for them, and it isn't any fun because they use it to

hurt people. I wish I didn't have to play anymore, but you can't stop because telling secrets can hurt people too. I don't know how to get out of it.

Chapter 18: The Purchase of Pond Street

The days leading up to the big meeting of the Pond Street residents, were lonely days for Karen. Davey wasn't much of an ally. He didn't want to talk, and every time they passed at school or on the bus, his eyes held such a look of fear and shame that she began to avoid him. Mr. Gunderson wasn't well enough to read to on Tuesday or Wednesday. Every time Karen came over, Mrs. Gunderson shook her head sadly and made her take the dollar. That wasn't what she wanted, but she couldn't say that to Mrs. Gunderson. And then there was her mother, who was always working. In the few hours when she wasn't, she seemed just as worried and withdrawn as Karen.

On Thursday, the sadness and fear that had been building, came sharply into focus. What if Mr. Gunderson could not attend the meeting that night? They had done so much together to bring it all to this point, but Karen had a sick feeling that the meeting might be a disaster if Mr. Gunderson wasn't there. Her fears twisted into a knot in her stomach when Mrs. Gunderson said that her husband could not do their reading that afternoon.

"He's saving his strength," she said with a hint of a smile. "He insists on attending that meeting tonight. I told him I'd go, but he wants to be there. Do you think we could get a ride with you and your mother?"

"Oh yes," Karen said in a flood of relief. "I'm sure that would be fine."

But she was worried again when she saw Mrs. Gunderson helping her husband across the yard to the Taylors' house that evening. His cheeks were sunken and he was very pale. He moved with an unsteady shuffle. His unseeing eyes looked straight ahead into the distance under a frown of heavy concentration, but he smiled readily when he heard Karen's voice.

"Mr. Gunderson, I'm so glad to see you. I was worried you would be too sick to go to the meeting."

"I'd have to be awfully sick for that, Karen. This is the payoff for all your hard work."

"It wasn't just Karen, Mr. Gunderson," Karen's mom said as they got in the car. "It was you, too."

"Nonsense," Mr. Gunderson said firmly. "Without Karen, none of this would have happened, and the people of this street would be a million dollars poorer."

"A million dollars," Karen's mother said, shaking her head in disbelief. "That's a lot of money."

"Not bad for a kid in sixth grade," Mr. Gunderson said with a laugh, and Karen was happier to hear that laugh than to hear about all those dollars.

The meeting took place in a large meeting room. There were chairs lined up in rows, facing a small stage that was about a foot higher than the floor. On the stage, there was a little stand, and behind it, three chairs sat facing out at the audience, where half the people of Pond Street were already seated. Karen noticed immediately that no other children were in the audience. The Carlsons were near the stage, but they'd left the twins home, probably with Jenny Stumpf babysitting. Karen's mother found four seats together, with one on the aisle for Mr. Gunderson, and they all sat down.

There was a mutter of quiet talk as everyone waited for the meeting to begin. Karen watched the faces and saw a generally open, trusting look. It was clear that none of them knew exactly what this was about, but they were hopeful. People kept coming in by ones and twos. Karen recognized nearly every one of them. The room was filling up, and the chatter was getting louder. Suddenly the Torvalds appeared in the doorway, and Davey was with them.

Karen stood up and waved. Davey saw her and held up a hand as inconspicuously as he could. Mr. Torvald looked the other way. Mrs. Torvald smiled and waved shyly. Karen felt a little more confident that she had done the right thing going to talk to them. The fact that she had – sort of - broken her promise of secrecy didn't seem to matter, since the mayor called that same afternoon. She had tried to help them as best she could. How could that be wrong?

Mayor Larson and Mr. Wilson came in through a side door and took their seats on the stage. Mr. Bellamy came in a moment later and sat beside them. The mayor looked around and decided it was time to start. He stood and stepped forward to the little stand, smiling.

"Good evening," he said loud enough to quiet the chatter. "I think I know everyone here, but in case some of you don't know me, I'm Dan Larson, your mayor. Before we get started, I want to introduce the people sitting up here behind me. First there's Joe Wilson from the bank." Mr. Wilson smiled and nodded, but Karen thought he looked a little nervous. "I think most of you know him," the mayor continued. "He's here representing the local business community to help you understand how important tonight's announcement is for the economic future of our town. And this is Jerry Bellamy, from a company called Townsend Investment Trust. Jerry and his company have some big plans for us, and I'm going to ask him to tell you about them now."

Mayor Larson sat down and Mr. Bellamy went up to the stand. His chubby face was a normal shade of pink, and his smile seemed natural enough until his gaze wandered over to Karen. Then his eyes seemed to narrow and the smile looked like it was painted on. Karen noticed, but she doubted whether anyone else did.

"Hello everybody," he said, and then he gave a boring introduction of himself and his company, calling it a development company and leaving out all the lies he'd told Karen's mom about their mission of helping homeowners in distress. Finally, he got to the point. "I know I've talked with a few of you about buying your homes. You might have wondered why I wanted them. Due to our client's need for secrecy, I couldn't tell you – until tonight. The fact is, I need to buy every single house on Pond Street. In order to make this a fair and open process, your mayor and I talked to the client and got their permission to tell you why we need your properties and to make an offer to each of you that I hope you will find too good to refuse."

A flurry of chatter erupted in the room. Mr. Bellamy paused until it died down. Then he talked about the terrible future Pine Springs faced due to the decline of the old furniture factory and announced the plan for a new "production facility for a major corporation" to be built out beyond Skinner's Swamp. He told them how the jobs and taxes the plant would bring would revitalize the town and make it prosperous again. This created another stir of excitement from the audience.

Mr. Seabloom raised his hand and stood up when Mr. Bellamy pointed to him. He asked who the plant was being built for, and Mr. Bellamy had to say that, for competitive reasons, the company didn't want that information given out.

Mr. Seabloom then asked what kind of business the plant would do, and Mr. Bellamy had to say that was being kept secret, too.

"Then how can we know," Mr. Seabloom asked, "if we can handle any of these new jobs?"

"Ah. That one I can answer," Mr. Bellamy smiled. "The jobs I'm talking about are not specialized or technical. These are general labor, clerical, and non-technical jobs that the company will train you for. They will be offered first to the residents of Pine Springs, and you will be given preference for them."

Mr. Seabloom nodded and said, "Thank you," and sat down.

Then Mr. Bellamy told them about the access road to be built on Pond Street and how he came up with the new offers for the homes along the street. There was a low murmur from the crowd as he described the new pricing and people started to see how much their homes could be worth. The offers would be good for one week, and a five percent deposit to bind the agreements would be paid when all of them were signed.

"You see, that's the main thing for my company. We need all of those agreements signed as soon as possible. Without them the project cannot move forward, which could mean the plant would be built in another town. That's why these offers are so generous. It's a once-in-a-lifetime opportunity for you. And it's absolutely critical for the future of this town. Any questions?"

Only old Mr. Vandergaard put up his hand. Mr. Bellamy pointed to him and he stood up slowly.

"What if we don't want to sell?" Mr. Vandergaard asked. His voice was raspy with age, but firm.

The question started a low murmur in the crowd, but this murmur had a different tone. There was a note of anger to it that hadn't been part of the earlier buzz. People frowned and turned in their seats to look at the old man.

Mr. Bellamy's smile suddenly seemed strained. "I hope when you see the numbers that won't be an issue," he said. "Joe Wilson, who helped me come up with these prices, knows the town much better than I do. He figures these offers are more than double what the properties would bring on the open market today. That should make them pretty hard to resist."

"Maybe for most of these folks," Mr. Vandergaard said, "but the money don't mean nothing to me. I'm 86 years old. I only got a few years left and I've lived in that shack my whole life. That's all I got, and it's all I want – just a few more years in my own home. After I'm gone, you can do whatever you want with it."

Mr. Vandergaard sat down and the murmur became stronger and angrier than before. Karen heard a woman's voice say the word, "selfish" quite clearly within the general mutter.

Mr. Gunderson rose slowly and painfully to his feet and turned toward Mr. Vandergaard, who sat to his right a few rows back. "Henry," he said in a weak voice, "I'm almost as old as you, and I've probably got less time left. I understand how you feel about the money, because I feel the same way. But I think we've got to look at this differently. Can we really say that our comfort for those few years is worth more than the chance for good jobs and a future for all our friends and neighbors in this town? I don't know about you, but I can't."

He sat down, exhausted, as a few people clapped and others said, "Right."

Mr. Vandergaard stood up again. His face was set in a stubborn frown. "Hal, I'll think about it, but the way I'm feeling, I'd rather you just shoot me right now and be done with it. That way you wouldn't need the nonsense of a big fancy deal for my old place."

The old man sat down and stared straight ahead, as if he wasn't hearing the angry hiss that rose up around him. Mr. Bellamy looked pained. "Now, Mr. ... uh, uh ... Mr. ..." he stammered.

"Vandergaard," the old man said firmly.

"Mr. Vandergaard. I hope you'll wait to see our offer and think about how much this means to all your neighbors before you decide."

"I said I'd think about it, didn't I?" Mr. Vandergaard snapped without getting up. "And you're a fine one to talk about how much this means to my neighbors when you tried to snatch up their property on the cheap."

Mayor Larson stood up. "Now, that's never been the plan. In a couple cases, Mr. Bellamy had to make preliminary offers to protect the project, but we never intended to carry through with those sales until the project could be announced and the prices adjusted, just as we're doing right now."

There weren't any more questions. Mr. Bellamy announced that he'd be giving out the Purchase and Sale offers to the homeowners on the way out, and he'd be available for questions by phone any time. He sat down looking tired and relieved at the same time. The mayor got up and said he thought this was a fine and a fair plan, and he hoped everyone would take advantage of it. He said they should drop off their signed agreements at his office some time within the next week and warned them not to talk about the project to anyone else in town. That could cause problems that might delay or even cancel the project. He thanked them all for coming and said good night. The meeting was over.

Mr. Bellamy went to the main door and started handing out manila envelopes to each family as they left. Mayor Larson stepped down into the crowd and started shaking hands and talking with people. Karen's little group waited for the crowd to move out before they got up, so that Mr. Gunderson didn't have to be on his feet too long. Karen turned to watch the Torvalds in the line moving toward the door. Mr. Torvald looked worried as came up to Mr. Bellamy and said something. Mr. Bellamy shuffled through the remaining envelopes and handed one to Mr. Torvald with a strained smile. Mr. Torvald seemed surprised. He cast a quick glance at Karen as they went out the door, his brows drawn together in a puzzled expression. Davey waved and managed a small smile.

When the crowd was gone, Mrs. Taylor and Mr. Gunderson got their envelopes from Mr. Bellamy. He said something stiff and formal to them, but he couldn't even look at Karen. She didn't notice. She was too aware of how slowly and weakly Mr. Gunderson shuffled along, leaning heavily on his wife's arm. When he got to the car, he dropped into the back seat like he couldn't go another step.

But he opened up the envelope and showed the papers to his wife, who then whispered in his ear. His tired face broke into a soft smile. "Looks like we all owe you a big thanks, Karen," he said. "Especially the Torvalds."

"It's only fair," Karen said.

"That's true," he agreed. When they'd gone a little further, he added, "You know their boy, don't you?"

"Oh, yeah," Karen said offhand. "I see him at school, but he's one of the popular kids."

"Well, I think you're going to be one of the popular kids now too, especially on Pond Street."

Chapter 19: Tough Choices

On Friday, at school, Davey was surrounded by his friends. He didn't try to talk to Karen, but he gave her a strange look when he got off the bus with Matt Talbot. He caught her eye for a half second longer than he needed to and the corners of his lips turned up with a hint of a smile, but his eyes were dark and serious. Karen liked having Davey as her secret ally, but she didn't know what that look meant, and it made her nervous.

After school, she went over to the Gunderson's. Mrs. Gunderson told her that Mr. Gunderson needed to rest after the big meeting. She said she hoped he would be strong enough for his regular reading hour on Monday.

Saturday, she sent off her message to Eva, as usual, but it seemed like there was so much she wasn't telling – the meeting with the mayor, Davey, the salamanders – somehow, it didn't relieve the cloud of isolation that suddenly seemed to surround her.

On Sunday, Davey came over after church and wanted to ride bikes again. He didn't say anything to explain the weird look he'd given her. In fact, he hardly said anything. He seemed kind of quiet and shy. Karen had the uncomfortable feeling that she didn't understand what was going on with him.

She didn't want to ride bikes because she wanted to be sure to be there when her mother got home from the diner. She suggested a walk in the woods instead. Davey shrugged and followed along. They crossed the swamp on the path and walked along the crest of the low hills to the flat rock.

Karen pointed out across the scrub covered hills. "That's where the new plant's going to go," she said seriously.

"If that old man doesn't stop it," Davey mumbled sullenly.

"You think he will?"

"I don't know, but my dad's already getting all messed up again." He sat down on the flat rock and stared at the ground between his feet. "It's not fair. Just when it looks like we've got something good, someone has to come along and ruin it."

"But we don't know, yet," Karen said hopefully, sitting down beside him. "He said he'd think about it. Maybe he'll change his mind."

"He better," Davey said bitterly.

They fell into a strained silence. Karen had her own worries about the new plant. It was complicated, and she didn't know what to do. She only knew that sitting and worrying about it wasn't going to help her solve the problem.

"Did you know that swamp has been there for a thousand years – maybe longer?" she asked, breaking the silence.

Davey looked up with a puzzled frown. "No."

"Well, it has. And there's a little salamander that lives down there that doesn't live anyplace else in the world."

"So?"

"So, we've got to make sure the plant doesn't ruin the swamp so the salamanders can't live there anymore."

"Who cares about a salamander? The plant is what's important. My dad's going to get a job there."

"I know, I know," Karen said. "But they can make it so the plant won't hurt the salamanders. We need to make sure they do."

"I don't care about that," Davey said angrily.

Karen didn't know what to make of Davey's strange mood, but she wasn't going to let it get in her way. "Come on," she said, starting down the hill. "Maybe if you see this little guy – we call him Newton - you'll understand."

Davey hung back for a few seconds, as if he didn't want to go along with her stupid idea, but when he saw she was halfway down the hill, he ran to catch up. After Karen explained how they would have to sneak up on the little brown salamander with the pink and yellow spotted back, Davey started to get into it. They both slogged through the mud eagerly searching the shallow water, and it was fun, for awhile.

But after an hour without any luck, both of them were getting discouraged. Karen was watching the time, and she was almost ready to give up and go home, when Davey, who was about 20 feet away on the bank of another small pond, suddenly put up his hand. He was staring intently at a spot a few feet in front of him. Karen moved slowly and quietly toward him.

When she was a few steps away, trying to follow Davey's gaze, she suddenly saw the brightly colored spots. It was Newton, or one of his cousins. The little black eyes were turned toward Davey as if the two of them were in a staring contest. The spotted body blended with the weeds along the bank and remained perfectly still as Karen moved slowly and silently to Davey's side.

Karen and Davey barely breathed. The salamander did not move at all for a full minute. Then, the little head suddenly turned away, and two seconds later, he shot into the water and slithered down to the murky bottom.

"Wow," Davey said. "I never saw one of those before."

"Almost nobody has," Karen said proudly. "This scientist that showed them to me said we were the first ones to ever see them."

"Really?"

"Yeah, and they're really important. She said they would be studying them for a long time. Come on, I've got to get back home."

They went up the hillside and started back. Davey seemed to be over his grumpy mood, but he was quiet as they walked. Every time Karen looked at him, he seemed to be deep in thought.

"Who's this scientist?" he asked when they were almost back to the path. "How come you know her?"

"There's two of them, Ron and Janice. I just met them out here by accident. They told me about the salamanders and how dangerous it would be for them if somebody built a plant here without protecting the swamp. But they don't know about the project. We're the only ones who know. So we've got to make sure they protect the swamp. Right?"

"I guess," Davey said uncertainly. "But what if they won't? Maybe they'd just move the plant somewhere else, and my dad wouldn't get a job. That would be worse."

"I know. What do you think we should do?"

"I don't know," Davey shrugged. "You're the one who always knows everything. You figure it out."

Karen was waiting on the front step when her mom got home. She had cleaned all the mud off her clothes. Her homework was done; the garden was weeded; the dishes were done, and the house was spotless. She wasn't going to let anything take up this precious time with her mother.

Karen felt like everyone was depending on her – her mother, Mr. Gunderson, Davey, the salamanders, Ron and Janice, and everybody on Pond Street. She was starting to think she might not be able to satisfy all of them. It was confusing, and it didn't seem fair. She wanted to just forget it and be a dumb little girl again. But that was the hard part about learning something. Once you knew, you couldn't just ignore it and pretend you didn't. You had to do something about it – at least Karen did – but sometimes it was confusing and exhausting. A nice afternoon with her mother would help.

Sunday afternoon was usually a quiet time. After a long week at the diner, Mrs. Taylor needed the rest. That would have been fine with Karen, but that Sunday, her mom had other plans.

"Let's have a little picnic," she said, hurrying out of her uniform and into a pair of jeans and a cotton pullover. "Help me make some sandwiches."

So they drove up onto the ridge and stopped at Lookout Park, a small meadow with some picnic tables and a fire pit. There were only two other groups at the park. Karen and her mother got a table where they could look down into the valley and see all of Pine Springs laid out below. Karen put their sandwiches on the table and poured some lemonade for herself and her mother.

They hadn't talked much on the ride up. Karen's mom seemed distracted, lost in thought, and Karen was comfortable with the silence. She knew that whatever was on her mother's mind would come out in due time.

"There it is," her mother said, putting down her sandwich and looking down at the town, "good old Pine Springs, a sleepy little town where nothing ever happens – until now. Now everything is going to change."

Karen looked down and saw the little town caught between the steep slope of the ridge and an interstate highway that looked like a thick double ribbon of traffic that mostly whizzed on past. The factory was quiet, slowly dying beside the town it had built and sustained. A few trucks were backed up to the loading docks, and a fork lift moved among the long buildings sided with rusty corrugated metal. Pond Street was an odd little tail that stuck out on the far side of the interstate, running straight down into the dark green heart of the swamp. Beyond that the low rolling hills of scrub gradually flattened out into farm land. Karen could see where the new plant would be, and from that height, it looked dangerously close to the fragile swamp.

"It's a good change, though, isn't it?" Karen said, more of a question than she intended.

"Yeah, I guess," her mom sighed. "Necessary, anyway. But it won't be the same … especially for us. That's what I wanted to talk to you about. We've got to start thinking where we'll go."

"What do you mean?"

"Well, when we get the money for the house, we could buy another place in town, or we could use it to go someplace else and start fresh."

"Do you want to go someplace else?" Karen asked, surprised.

"I don't know. I guess I'm getting tired of working at the diner all the time and not making enough to pay the bills."

"You could get a job at the new plant. Mr. Bellamy said they'd train you."

"You think so? I never did anything but waitress. That doesn't prepare you for much."

"There it is ... good old Pine Springs."

"I bet you could get a better job there, and you'd have normal hours, too."

"That'd be nice," Karen's mom said wistfully. "The thing is, if we're ever going to go anywhere and try anything new, now would be the time."

"We don't need to go anywhere to try something new. There's going to be new stuff right here."

"Maybe. So then it comes down to – do we like Pine Springs? Do we want to stay?"

"Of course we do. It's our home. We know people. Anyplace else we'd just be strangers. Why would we want to leave?"

"I don't know. Sometimes I think we're just stuck. The world is rushing by, and we're stuck in this little nowhere town, afraid to poke our heads out and see what's going on out there."

She was silent for a moment, gazing out over the town to where cloud shadows moved slowly in formation across the prairie. "There's so many memories here," she sighed. "They don't let you move on. Maybe that's why we're stuck."

"But they're good memories, aren't they?" Karen asked tentatively.

Mrs. Taylor turned to her and smiled. Karen could see where a tear had rolled down her cheek and left a wet streak. Her mother wiped it away with the back of her hand. "Yes they are," she said. "They're very good memories."

Chapter 20: Her Neighbors' Thanks

After school on Monday, Karen hurried straight over to the Gundersons'. She had not seen Mr. Gunderson since the meeting, and she was worried he still would not be strong enough for their reading. She had so much on her mind, she was hoping he could help her with some of it.

At the door, Mrs. Gunderson was quiet and serious, not as cheerful as she usually was. "I didn't want him to get up today at all," she said. "He's still weak, but he said he had a couple things he had to talk to you about. Try to cut it short today, and don't let him get excited."

"I won't," Karen promised, realizing that she could not bring up some of the things that were bothering her.

Mr. Gunderson was sitting in his usual spot, but he did not look well. His face was drawn and pale and his head rested limply against the high back of the chair.

"Hello, Karen," he said, but even his voice sounded tired.

"Hello, Mr. Gunderson. How are you?" Karen hadn't meant to ask that, but it was the thought that was foremost in her mind, and it just came out, like they always did.

"Well, I guess I'm a little worn out right now. These meetings seem to use up all my energy."

"Maybe you shouldn't have gone. I'm sure the mayor would have understood if you said you weren't well enough."

"Oh, no," Mr. Gunderson smiled weakly. "I wouldn't have missed it for the world. You know, you should have been the hero at that meeting."

"Why?" Karen asked, surprised. "I didn't do anything."

"If they only knew how it all happened, I'm sure the people on this street would disagree. Without you, they'd be a million dollars poorer. Unfortunately, the mayor was right.

We couldn't let them know that he and Mr. Bellamy were trying to cheat them. It would just add to the risk that someone would try to hold things up. So, we've got to let them take the credit that should really go to you."

"Is that why the mayor kept saying the meeting never happened?"

"Exactly."

"I guess I didn't get that."

"Kind of makes you mad, doesn't it?"

Karen shrugged. "Not really. I don't care who gets credit, so long as we end up doing the right thing."

"You're right, Karen." He let his head fall back against the cushions with a tired sigh. "It really doesn't matter, does it?"

His breathing was slow and shallow, making a kind of shushing sound in his throat. Karen thought he had gone to sleep, but, without raising his head, he suddenly said, "Is everybody happy with Mr. Bellamy's offers?"

"I think so. I talked to a bunch of the kids yesterday, and they all said their parents were going to sign."

"Good. I'm sure your mother's happy, too."

"Well ..." Karen said, uncertainly.

"What?" Mr. Gunderson was surprised enough to lift his head. "I'm sure it was a good price."

"Oh yes, it was. It's just that my mom is kind of attached to our house. She sees it like it's part of my dad. I'm sure she'll sign, but she's still kind of sad about it."

Mr. Gunderson smiled weakly. "I understand. I think we all feel that way. If it wasn't for the money – and what it means to the town – I don't think any of us would be moving away."

"It's our home," Karen said, thinking of the salamanders.

"That's right. I don't suppose you've heard anything about what Mr. Vandergaard's going to do?"

"No. I hardly ever see him."

"I'm worried about him. He could put a stop to this whole thing."

"Do you think he'd really do that? You told him how selfish that would be."

"I tried, but I'm not sure it was enough. Henry is the kind who doesn't depend on anybody and doesn't want anybody depending on him. We're asking him to make a big sacrifice for us."

"But what do we do if he won't sign?"

"We've got to make him change his mind."

"How?"

Mr. Gunderson's head fell back again and he smiled up at the ceiling. "Well," he said softly, "you're pretty good at changing minds, "I was hoping you'd have some ideas."

He fell asleep in his chair soon after that.

Karen was disappointed but not surprised the next afternoon, when Mrs. Gunderson told her that Mr. Gunderson couldn't have his reading that day. She walked back across the weedy lawn to her front door, with a weight of worry on her narrow shoulders that was all about Mr. Gunderson. She dropped her books on the table and flopped on the couch with so many scary thoughts flying through her head that it all seemed to blend into nothing, a big black hole that threatened to swallow her up.

Mrs. Taylor got home a few minutes later. It was her night off, and she was surprised to find Karen lying on the couch. "Hi, Sweetie," she said with some concern. "What's the matter? Don't you feel well?"

"Mr. Gunderson's sick."

"Oh." Karen's mom stood over her in her waitress uniform with a look of sadness softening her pretty face. "You know, he's been sick for a long time, and sometimes it's worse than others. He'll probably be better in a few days."

"Maybe. But he's so old and weak, and he gets tired so easy. It must be hard for him."

"I know. And it's hard for us, who are young and healthy, to see our friends get like that, isn't it?"

"It's awful," Karen said with a choke in her voice. "It's not fair."

Her mother sat down beside her and put a soft hand on her shoulder. "No. It's not."

A few minutes later, there was a knock on the door. Karen ran to her room while her mother went to see who it was. Karen lay on her bed, hardly aware of the voices in the front room. She wanted to cry, to throw off the heavy blanket of sadness that had wrapped itself around her heart, but she couldn't. All she could do was stare into the black hole and wait for it to take her away.

"Karen. Karen, could you come in here for a minute?"

It was her mother's voice, calling her back into the world. Karen got up and looked quickly into the mirror. The deep brown eyes that looked back at her were too sad. She blinked once or twice and took a deep breath, then walked out to the front room, where her mother and Mrs. Torvald and Mrs. Carlson were sitting around the coffee table.

"Honey," her mother smiled, "Mrs. Carlson and Mrs. Torvald stopped by to say thank you."

"Oh." Karen stood on the other side of the coffee table, her face blank, as if she'd just awakened from a deep sleep and couldn't yet figure out where she was or what was going on.

"Yes," Mrs. Carlson said. "We were very surprised and we didn't understand what you were doing when you came by our house that night two weeks ago to warn us about Mr. Bellamy. It seemed very strange and ... and not like you. We didn't know what to think."

"I know," Karen said. "I shouldn't have done that. I'm sorry."

"Don't be sorry," Mrs. Torvald said. "Now we understand. And we think what you did was wonderful. That's why we're here, to thank you."

"Thank me?" Karen said, still confused.

"Yes. Very much." Mrs. Torvald's eyes were shining on Karen. "Your mother couldn't tell us how it happened, and we don't need to know, but we do know that what you did, you did for us. It was a wise and caring thing to do, way beyond your years, Karen, and we're lucky to have you for a neighbor."

Karen was speechless. She stared at the three women, smiling across the coffee table at her. The pride that glowed in her mother's face was too much. It felt as if the heavy blanket around her heart had suddenly burst, and the tears started from her eyes. "I ... I just ... You're welcome." She sobbed and ran back into her room and threw herself on the bed. Her tears soaked into the bedspread, but the black hole was gone.

"She's very worried about our neighbor, Mr. Gunderson," Karen heard her mother explain. "Karen reads to him some afternoons, and he's been very ill. You know, I think he helped Karen understand some of this business about the development project. He probably deserves our thanks, too."

"I thought so," Mrs. Carlson said. "When I saw him with you at the meeting and he got up to say what he did to old Mr. Vandergaard, it seemed like he had a very good idea of what was going on."

"That's true," Mrs. Torvald added. "I think he said what we were all feeling. I just hope it got through to that stubborn old man. I don't know what will happen now if he stops this project."

"I don't either," Mrs. Carlson agreed. "We live next door to him, and we hardly know him. If Hal Gunderson couldn't change his mind, I don't think the mayor or that Mr. Bellamy are going to have much luck."

Chapter 21: The Grownup World

The next day, when Mrs. Gunderson answered Karen's knock, she was pale and trembling. She had a tissue in her hand and she had been crying. Karen immediately feared the worst.

"Mr. Gunderson," she choked, turning pale herself. "Is he … is he alright?"

"Oh, yes dear. Thank you," Mrs. Gunderson said, managing a weak smile. "He's a little better today – not well enough to get up for his reading, yet, but perhaps in a few days."

"But, what's wrong?" Karen asked before she realized the question might be impertinent.

Mrs. Gunderson did not seem to mind. She pulled the front door shut behind her and came out onto the front step with Karen. "I've been so upset," she said, leaning against the rusty metal rail. "I know I should be stronger, but with Mr. Gunderson so ill, I feel so vulnerable." The old lady paused for a moment, looking earnestly into Karen's eyes. "If I tell you something, will you promise not to talk about it with Mr. Gunderson? I'm afraid it would make him so angry it would be dangerous to his fragile health."

"I promise."

"That man came by today, that Mr. Bellamy."

"He came here, too?" Karen said, shocked.

"Yes. I haven't taken those papers over to the mayor's office yet, and he wanted to know if we had any questions – well, that's what he said at first. He was very polite and friendly, but that was just an act."

"Why? What do you mean?"

"What he really wanted was for Mr. Gunderson to talk to Mr. Vandergaard again, to try to convince him to sign the papers. He and the mayor had tried to talk to him and Mr. Vandergaard refused to sign. It could be a very big problem for this project and for the town."

"I know."

"Well, I couldn't let him talk to Mr. Gunderson - with him so sick. That made him very angry. His face got all red and he talked loud, almost shouting. I was deathly afraid he would wake Mr. Gunderson."

Karen's face clenched in an angry frown. "That's terrible."

"Yes it was. He said all kinds of nasty things. We were a 'bunch of ignorant country bumpkins' who didn't understand how important this project was. Mr. Gunderson thought he had beaten him by getting a better price for our 'pathetic little street'. I've never seen such rudeness, never been so insulted. It would have made me mad if I hadn't been so afraid."

"He's just a big fat bully," Karen exploded.

"I think that's a very good description. But I'm terrified that he'll come back. Mr. Gunderson just isn't strong enough to stand that."

"I know," Karen sighed. "I wish there was something I could do to help."

Mrs. Gunderson's weak smile returned, a little stronger this time. "You know, my dear, I think you already have. I felt so alone until you came to the door. Just talking it over with you has made me feel stronger. I think I'll call up the mayor and give him a piece of my mind. He needs to control that man, and I'm going to tell him so."

"That's a wonderful idea, Mrs. Gunderson. We shouldn't have to be afraid in our own homes."

"No we shouldn't," the old lady said, turning her soft wrinkled face to take in all of Pond Street, "even if they may not be ours much longer."

Karen went home and did her homework, although she found it hard to concentrate. Other thoughts kept creeping into her head. When she was done, she looked around the house, hoping to lose herself in some housework, but the house was already neat and clean, and the dishes were done. She went into the garden and couldn't find any weeds. She went back in the house and plopped down on the couch, feeling useless and fidgety.

After two minutes, she popped up again and went to the window. Sunlight streamed down through the trees. Off in the distance, the swamp was a deep green shadow. She threw off her school clothes and put on a T-shirt, jeans, and her old hiking boots. Then she was out the door and tromping down the path.

She got to the flat rock and sat there for a few minutes looking down at the ponds that were home to the salamanders. She wondered if they would fight for their homes the way old Mr. Vandergaard did. The difference was that they had no power to fight the people who threatened them. Those people might kill them, wipe out every last one, and never even know they had done it. The world was so unfair.

She went down into the swamp to see if she could spot one. In the first pond she came to, she saw something that puzzled her at first. There were several tiny creatures swimming around in the shallow water. They seemed to have the salamander's brown back, without the colorful spots, and their legs were much smaller. They looked a little like tadpoles, but longer and thinner, with some kind of spiky growths coming out of their heads. Also, unlike Newton, they stayed in the water and never came up for air. She watched them for a long time before she realized what they were. They were salamander babies. She was almost sure of it. She went to several more ponds, and all of them had little salamander babies swimming around in them.

Karen wished that Ron and Janice were there to see them. She knew they'd be excited, but they weren't coming back until Sunday. That was too long to wait. On the other hand, Karen knew she'd have to make a decision by then, so maybe it wasn't long enough. As dusk began to fall, she walked home worried and confused. This time she didn't wait for bedtime to share her thoughts with Eva. She went straight into her bedroom and wrote:

> I think I'm going crazy. There are too many things that need to be done, and they're all going off in different directions. It's like I'm being torn in pieces. Mr. Gunderson is very sick, but it seems like he is the only one who can rescue our street and our town from drying up and blowing away. I want to help but I don't know how. And then, there's old Mr. Vandergaard (do you remember him?). He's part of the problem, but all he's asking is to be left alone. That doesn't seem like too much to ask.

> I haven't even told you about what could be the biggest problem of them all. I can't talk about it yet, not until I decide what to do. It's just another big secret. All of a sudden, it

seems like everything is a secret, and everybody's got something they want from somebody else. If this is the grownup world, I don't know how grownups survive.

Chapter 22: Mr. Vandergaard

At recess the next day, Davey caught Karen's eye and led her to their spot behind the corner of the school building. He was scared and breathless. "We've got to do something. My dad is so mad at Mr. Vandergaard he's swearing and banging his fist against the wall, talking crazy. I'm afraid he might do something bad."

"I know. Everybody's worried. But what can we do?"

"I don't know. We've just got to get Mr. Vandergaard to sign that paper."

"But how?"

"I don't know. I don't know," Davey wailed. "I just know we've got to do it. We can't let my Dad get himself in trouble."

"Alright. I'll try to think of something."

"Okay, but it's got to be today. Right? Those papers are supposed to be turned in by tomorrow. If Mr. Vandergaard doesn't … I don't know. My dad might … After tonight, it might be too late."

After school, on the bus home, Davey's eyes again pleaded with her, but Karen had already made up her mind. She was glad that Davey sat with his friends and they couldn't talk. All her thoughts were concentrated on what she would say to Mr. Vandergaard. It seemed like everything she thought of had already been said. When she arrived at Mr. Vandergaard's front step, she still had no plan beyond knocking on his door.

Then, as soon as she knocked, a horrible thought came into her head. What if he was angry? Everybody had been pushing at him, talking behind his back. Maybe he knew, and maybe he was mad about it. Would he open the door and yell at her, chase her away? She had been so focused on ways to make him change his mind she hadn't even considered the possibility that he might be angry or mean.

The door opened and the old man stood behind the screen. He didn't look angry. He looked surprised and maybe a little pleased. "Oh, hello Karen," he said mildly.

"Hello Mr. Vandergaard," Karen said, relieved. "I wonder if I could talk to you for a few minutes about ... well, about signing the paper, you know, to sell your house."

"Sure, sure. Come on in."

He led her into the kitchen and pulled a chair out from the kitchen table. Barney, the old dog with the reddish coat and the white muzzle, wandered in and dropped on the floor beside her, sighing comfortably. "Here," Mr. Vandergaard said. "Would you like something to drink? I've got iced tea or ... um, water. I don't drink much soda pop, so I guess I don't have much call to keep it around."

"Oh, thank you. A glass of water would be nice."

Mr. Vandergaard filled a glass and brought it to the table. He sat down across from her and smiled as she took a sip. "I'm glad it was you that came this time. When the mayor and that Mr. Bellamy came by they made me so mad I wanted to throw them both out on the street. Good thing I'm not young and strong anymore, or I might've."

"I guess I don't blame you. Mr. Bellamy is pretty rude."

"Ah," the old man snorted, "the mayor isn't much better. He kept telling me how important it was for the town and all the people in it, how my father helped build this town and he'd want me to sign so it didn't turn into a ghost town. Now, how would he know what my father would want? My daddy was dead before the mayor was even born."

"Your father helped build this town?"

"He sure did – almost a hundred years ago. When he came out here, there was nothing but a few shacks, a farm store, and a general store for the miners looking for silver up in the hills. Then old Mr. Peabody started making furniture, and he had more and more people coming out to work in his factory. Those people needed houses and my father was a carpenter, so he had plenty of work. I bet he had his hand in half the houses on Main Street."

"Wow."

"Yeah, but you're not here for a history lesson, are you?" Mr. Vandergaard laughed, holding up Mr. Bellamy's offer sheets. "This is what you want, just like everybody else on the street."

"I guess so," Karen admitted.

"Okay, let me try to explain how I feel about it. First off, the money doesn't mean anything to me. I don't care if it's half this much or twice. My father built this house out here when there wasn't any Pond Street, and I never lived anyplace else. It just doesn't seem right I should have to move on for the last few years of my life just so some darn corporation can run a road across my property."

Karen looked up and saw the old man watching her with a sad, puzzled look in his eyes, almost as if it was a question. "No," she said, shaking her head, "it doesn't."

"But then there's the whole street, the whole town that's depending on it, huh?"

"That's true too," Karen said softly.

"Boy they sure knew what they were doing when they sent you to talk to me. I kept thinking it would be somebody else, maybe a bunch of them, maybe with baseball bats to pound some sense into this hard old head of mine."

"That wouldn't do any good, would it?" Karen said.

"No, it sure wouldn't. I can be as stubborn as a mule, especially when somebody's trying to push me."

"I didn't think I could push you, but I was hoping I could find a way to make you change your mind."

The old man shook his head sadly. "I'm afraid not, Karen. Only way to get this property out from under me is just shoot me. I can't give it up on my own. That'd be like shooting myself. My life is here, right here, on this little patch of earth. You take me away from it, you're taking away my life."

"I kind of understand that," Karen said. "It's like the rest of us feel about Pine Springs. We don't want to leave any more than you do. But without that plant, we can't stay. I guess we all think it's worth it to move over into town – better than moving to some strange place."

Mr. Vandergaard was silent for a long pause. He stared at his hands, rough and bent and folded before him on the table, but he didn't seem to see them. His eyes were seeing something far away, almost like Mr. Gunderson's. "Come with me, child," he finally said. "I want to show you something."

They walked down a short hall and Mr. Vandergaard opened a door. "Go ahead," he said. "Go on in."

Karen entered the room, which was dimly lit and smelled a little musty. It was a small room, mostly taken up with a high double bed. A faded quilt was spread over the bed and two fluffy pillows lay at the head, side by side. There was an old-fashioned dresser just across from the foot of the bed. On top of the dresser, there were two pictures in gold lacquered frames, a small hand mirror, and a hair brush. The mirror and the brush had fancy painted ceramic handles. On the floor there were two oval, hand-braided rugs made from rags of many colors. Two small windows looked out to a back yard with flowers and well-trimmed bushes. Sunlight streamed down through the trees, making it look like a little picture of paradise. There was a wooden chair and a small table by the windows.

Mr. Vandergaard stood in the doorway. "This was our room, me and Willa's," he said. "That's us in those pictures. We couldn't have any kids. We just had each other. She was taken from me long before you were born, and it was so sudden, I never got a chance to say goodbye. Maybe that would have made a difference. Anyway, when I came home from the hospital, I couldn't sleep in this room. I made myself a pallet in the other room and left this one the way it was. I kept telling myself to clear out her things, look ahead, try to forget, but I couldn't do it then, and I can't do it now. I come in here every day to talk to her."

Karen looked at the two pictures. One of them showed a young couple standing ankle deep in a gentle surf. They wore old-fashioned bathing suits and seemed to be posing. Only their wide, open-hearted smiles redeemed their stiff positioning. In the other picture, they were older, still posing formally. Mr. Vandergaard was recognizable, and Mrs. Vandergaard was a pleasant blond woman of about fifty. "You talk to her?" she questioned gently.

"I do."

"What does she say about selling your house?"

"I talk to her, Karen," he sighed, "but she can't talk to me."

It was Mrs. Taylor's night off. She was home, sitting back on the couch with her feet up on the coffee table, still wearing the neat tan and white dress that was her uniform at the diner, when Karen burst through the door.

"Come on, Mom," she said breathlessly. "There's someone I want you to talk to."

"What? Oh, Karen, I'm tired. Let me rest a few minutes."

"Not now. This is important," Karen said, catching her hand and pulling her to her feet. "Come on."

Karen dragged her mother up the street to Mr. Vandergaard's house.

As they walked up to the front door, Mrs. Taylor whispered, "What are we doing here?"

"I had a talk with Mr. Vandergaard – about signing the papers. But it's not me he needs to talk to, Mom. It's you."

Mr. Vandergaard opened the door. "Hello, Elaine," he said. "I see Karen's brought reinforcements."

Mrs. Taylor mumbled "Hello," but she looked quite bewildered.

"Mr. Vandergaard," Karen interrupted, "would you show my mom what you showed me. I think she'll understand."

"Okay," he said somewhat reluctantly. "Come in."

"I've got to get home and do my homework," Karen said. "You go, Mom. I'll see you at home. Bye Mr. Vandergaard."

Chapter 23: Close Call

Karen tried to do her homework, but she couldn't concentrate. She kept imagining what her mother and Mr. Vandergaard might be talking about. As the minutes crept by, she felt better and better about what she'd done, but she still felt very uncertain about the outcome. Her mother was gone for more than an hour.

When Mrs. Taylor came home, she still looked bewildered. Her eyes were red and she carried a piece of paper in her hand. She went to the table and dropped heavily into a chair. "He's such a nice old man," she said with a little choke in her voice. "I never knew."

"Did he sign it, Mom," Karen asked eagerly. "Is that the paper?"

Her mother looked at the paper in her hand. "Yes, he did, Sweetheart. He said he did it for you."

"Oh, he's wonderful," Karen laughed, "and so are you."

Karen looked out the window and saw twilight coming down on Pond Street. She raced to the door. "I got to go now. I'll be back in half an hour."

Her mother stood up. "Wait, Karen. Where …?"

But Karen was already running up the street. Her mother went to the door and watched her, more confused than ever.

Mrs. Torvald answered the door. She looked very worried and flustered. "Oh, Karen," she said. "I … um … I'll get Davey." She started back down the hall, then turned and swung the door almost shut in Karen's face.

Karen was a bit surprised at Mrs. Torvald's uncharacteristic rudeness, especially after the last time she had seen her, when she had been so warm and friendly. But she knew there was a lot of anger and upset in the Torvald home. That's why she was there. She heard the sound of a muffled argument. Mr. Torvald's voice sounded like distant thunder.

It took a long time for Davey to come to the door. When he did, his face was set in a hard and hopeless expression. He didn't open the screen door. "Go away," he said. "You can't come in."

"Davey, what's the matter? I've got good news. Mr. Vandergaard signed the paper."

"What? He did?" Suddenly a look of wonder and excitement flooded back into Davey's face. "You sure?"

"My mother's got the paper. I saw the signature."

"That's fantastic," he said, shoving the screen door open and nearly knocking Karen off the step. "Come on. We've got to tell my dad."

Davey ran ahead down the hall to the kitchen, as Karen followed timidly into the house. "Dad, Dad, Mr. Vandergaard signed," Davey yelled.

Karen entered the kitchen and Mr. Torvald jumped up from the table. "What the ..." he snarled. "I told you she couldn't come in."

Mr. Torvald looked wild. His cheeks and chin were dark with stubbly beard. His eyes were red and his hair stood out in tufts. He wore a stained white T-shirt and worn blue jeans. A can of beer was open on the table in front of him, but Karen hardly noticed any of that. All she saw was the big red can with a flexible spout that sat on the floor behind him. It was the kind of can she had seen people use to put gasoline in their lawn mowers.

Mr. Torvald lunged at Davey, as if to grab him.

Davey jumped away. "But Dad," he cried, "he signed. He signed."

Mr. Torvald stood in the middle of the kitchen floor, looking at Karen with a strange, uncomprehending look in his eyes. He seemed to sway a little from side to side. "What?" he said.

"He signed. Mr. Vandergaard signed the papers. Karen saw it."

Mr. Torvald looked from Davey to Karen with a fierce scowl. "Is that true?" he asked suspiciously. His mouth seemed stiff and thick around the words.

"It's true," Karen managed to squeak, still staring at the gas can. "My mom talked to him."

"Huh," he said, shaking his head, as if he didn't quite know what to do with the information.

Then he noticed where Karen was staring. He looked from the gas can to Karen and then to Davey. His mouth turned down in a scowl so fierce, it looked like he had just bitten into something horribly bitter. "What are you looking at?"

"Nothing, Dad."

"She is," he said, pointing a wavering finger at Karen. "You all think you know what's going on, and I'm just a stupid drunk. Well I know better than all of you. I know what to do when somebody gets in my way. You understand? I can take care of this myself. I don't need any help from some snotty little girl. Now get out of here, all of you. You make me sick."

He slumped down into the chair and laid his face on his arms on the table. He sat crumpled over the table, breathing hard, as if he'd just run a long way. Mrs. Torvald came into the room and stood beside Karen, looking down at her husband with a tortured expression. Karen felt very

All she saw was the big red can ... the kind of can
she had seen people use to put gasoline in their
lawn mowers.

uncomfortable, but she couldn't move. She was afraid that anything she did might make it worse.

"Pathetic," Mrs. Torvald said with deep disgust. She picked up the beer can and dumped what was left in the sink. Mr. Torvald didn't stir. "You drink yourself into a rage to let off steam. I hope you finally see how ugly and awful it is for the rest of us to watch you."

Mr. Torvald rolled his head on his arms to look up at her. "Get out," he said. His eyes were slits. "Just get out."

Suddenly Davey ran from the room and pounded up the stairs.

Mrs. Torvald walked Karen to the door. "I'm ver y sorry you had to see this," she said. "I don't know what we're going to do. We've got to hope he can get a job soon. Maybe that will help. For now, I know I've got no right to ask this, but please don't tell anyone what you saw. I don't know if I could live in this town if people knew."

"I won't tell anyone, Mrs. Torvald. I promise."

"Thank you," she said quietly. "I don't know how we can ever thank you enough."

"I don't … You don't have to," Karen said, almost too softly for Mrs. Torvald to hear as she shut the door.

Chapter 24: Bowling

"Well, that sure wasn't much," Karen's mom said when she got home about 9:30 the next night. She dropped her purse on the table and sank into her chair.

Karen sat in her own chair across the table. She was in her pajamas, having just had her bath. "What wasn't?" she asked.

"After all that talk about Mr. Vandergaard signing his offer ... When I brought in the signed sheets, the mayor's secretary barely said 'thanks'. She put them in a file, and that was it."

"Was the mayor there? Or Mr. Bellamy?"

"I didn't see them."

"Maybe they were busy with something else."

"I guess," Mrs. Taylor said, frowning. "It just seems like, with how important this is and everything, you'd think there'd be a little more excitement about it. And then, what you did to get those papers signed. That was amazing, and it looks like you're not getting any credit ... again."

"Oh, that's alright. It was you that did it anyway. But let's not tell people about any of that, okay? Maybe it would be embarrassing to Mr. Vandergaard. I don't know if he'd like people to know about that room."

"Oh yeah. I hadn't thought of that. Maybe you're right."

Davey came over on Saturday. Karen went out and sat on the front step. He sat beside her, but not too close. He was acting weird again, very quiet and solemn. After he said hello, he couldn't seem to think of anything else to say.

"How's your dad?" Karen asked. Davey's silence made her nervous.

"He's okay," Davey said.

"Is he going to try to get one of those construction jobs building the new plant?"

"I guess."

Karen tried again. "Just a few more weeks till summer vacation."

"19 more days." Davey was a little more enthusiastic this time.

"I guess we'll all be busy moving, then."

"Yeah."

"You know where you're going?"

"No."

Davey couldn't seem to sit still. His feet kept moving around and he kept wiping his hands on his pants, as if they were wet.

"What do you want to do?" Karen asked.

"Um, I don't know."

"You want to ride bikes?"

"Okay," Davey said, adding quickly, "we could ride over to the bowling alley and bowl some."

"I can't. I don't have any money."

"That's okay. I'll pay."

"Really?"

"Yeah."

"That's awfully nice of you. Are you sure you want to?"

"I'm sure." Davey said looking at her solemnly. "Let's go."

Karen kept her eyes and her mind on the traffic while they were on the county road until they were through the tunnel under the interstate. After that, as she pedaled, her mind was spinning as fast as her wheels. *Does Davey want to do this, or did his mother make him?* she wondered. When they got to the bowling alley, she still hadn't come up with an answer.

Davey went to the booth and got the shoes and the scorecard, while Karen searched for the lightest ball with the smallest finger holes. She found one that fit pretty well and joined Davey on the bench at one of the lanes. They changed their shoes and put the score sheet on the little table.

"You go first," Davey said.

Karen had bowled a few times before, but she wasn't very good. At least she didn't have to roll the ball with both hands any more. She could feel Davey watching her, and she wanted to look like she knew what she was doing. She took her four steps and let the ball go. It bounced once before it settled down and rolled slowly down the alley. It looked like it might be a gutter ball, but it held on long enough to knock down one pin.

She covered her face with her hands as she walked back to the bench. "Oh, that was terrible," she said.

"That's alright," Davey said encouragingly. "You're just getting warmed up. Try standing a little more to the left. It might help straighten out your line."

"Okay."

Karen tried it, and it worked. The ball went a little too far to the other side, and missed the head pin by an inch or two, but she knocked down another five pins, which wasn't too bad.

"Good ball," Davey commented.

When Davey rolled his first ball, it knocked down seven pins right out of the middle. Two pins were left standing at the right corner and one at the left.

Davey came back to the bench grinning. "Oh-oh, a split," he said. "I can never get these."

He rolled his second ball down the right side and it looked like it might go right through the middle, but it inched over enough to tick the inside pin, which flew off to the side, knocking down the other pin on the right. Then it bounced off the wall and came back across, spinning on its side. It tapped the pin on the left just hard enough to make it wobble and fall.

Davey jumped in the air, waving his arms. "I got it. I got the split."

"Wow," Karen said when he came back to the bench. "I didn't know you could do that."

"Well," Davey said modestly, "that's not really the way you're supposed to do it, but it worked."

After that, Davey was his old self, laughing and commenting on everything. He helped Karen a lot, and she started doing better. Near the end of the first game, she got a strike, which got her score up to 82. Davey got two strikes in the game and ended up with a score of 144.

"You want to bowl another game?" he asked.

"Sure," Karen said, "but that's expensive."

"It's not that bad. You want to get a drink first?"

"Wow," Karen laughed. "You must be rich."

They went to the counter and Davey ordered two root beers. They took them back to their lane and bowled another game. Davey started trying too hard and his score dropped slightly to 137, but he kept helping Karen, and she scored her best ever – 107. She told him he was a great coach and she needed him to help her whenever she bowled.

"That'd be great," he said enthusiastically, but quickly corrected himself. "I mean, I always like to go bowling."

"Me too," Karen said.

They rode home and stopped in front of Davey's house.

"See you Monday," Davey said.

Karen stood straddling her bike. "See you. And thanks, Davey. That was fun."

"Yeah."

She watched him walk his bike up the gravel driveway. *Was that a date?* she wondered.

Chapter 25: No Choice

Sunday after church, Karen walked out into her back yard and stood beside her neat little garden, looking up through the trees. The sky was dark and heavy over the deeper darkness of the swamp, giving it a sullen, unfriendly look. The damp, fresh smell of rain about to fall was thick in the air. If she went out to the swamp, she would probably get caught in the downpour. Maybe the threat of rain would keep Ron and Janice away, anyway. Going out there might be a complete waste of time. It would be a good afternoon to curl up on the couch and read a book.

But Karen knew it wasn't the weather that put those thoughts in her head. The real problem was that she didn't want to face a decision that seemed to have no good answer. But avoiding it was not the answer either. She tromped off down the path with a grim expression.

Ron and Janice were sitting on the flat rock, waiting. Ron's pack and two green plastic rain slickers lay on the rock beside him. "I thought you might not come today," he said. "Looks like rain."

"I had to," Karen said seriously. "There's millions of these little swimming things in the ponds down there. I saw them a few days ago, and I want to find out what they are. I thought they might be salamander babies. Do you think so?"

"I hope so," Janice said eagerly. "That's part of what we need for the report. Can you show me where you saw them?"

They went down into the swamp and started searching the ponds. Karen couldn't find any of the long skinny tadpoles for a few minutes. Then she saw two of them swimming in a shallow clear pool. She held up her hand and Ron came over to check it out.

"There," Karen said, pointing.

Ron watched the two creatures for a moment, before they suddenly darted into the weeds and were gone. "That's them." He sounded happy and excited. "We've got to catch one and take it back to the lab. You want to help?"

"Okay."

Ron got a clear plastic container out of his pack, filled it with water from the pond, and found a long stick for Karen. Janice had a net ready, and she stood with Ron over the clear pool where Karen had seen the two baby salamanders. Karen went around to the opposite bank of the pond. On Janice's signal, she began to thrash the stick around in the weedy sections of the pond. Janice watched the pool intently for a minute or two, then made a lunge with her net but came up empty.

On the second try, she got one in the net, but she didn't take it out of the water. Instead, Ron slid the container under the side of the net and used it to catch the swiftly zig-zagging young salamander. Karen ran around the pond and looked into the container.

"Wow, he's different than just a few days ago," Karen said, amazed. "His legs are longer and he's bigger."

"They grow pretty fast at this stage," Janice said.

"Yeah, but there were a lot more of them a few days ago. Where did they all go?"

"Most of them got eaten," Ron said. "They make a great meal for the frogs and snakes. Out of a couple hundred, only one or two live long enough to grow up."

"Oh." Karen was silent for a moment. "Is that why they're endangered?"

"No. That's just the normal balance of life in the swamp. From what I've seen, the population seems pretty stable. The only reason they might be considered endangered is that they don't live anywhere else. That means that anything that threatens their home here in the swamp could mean the end for them."

"But you could do something to protect them. Right?"

"Right." He held up the container with the little salamander swimming around in it. "This guy's going to help. When we've got all the results from the lab, we'll be ready to send around a paper about the new species. Then we can go to the state and federal wildlife agencies and get them recognized as endangered or threatened. That will mean that anyone who wants to do development or logging, or anything that might affect the swamp will have to prove they won't be hurting the salamanders."

"But that takes a long time, huh?"

"Too long," Janice said with some irritation.

"A few years," Ron said more evenly. "Why? Are you worried someone might come along and do something before then?"

"Well, what if they did? What could we do then?"

"Then it would be a little more complicated. We'd have to try to get the state to stop it - probably have to go to court."

"You mean before they built it, or after?"

"It's easier if they're still in the planning stages. Once they start construction, it gets much harder to stop."

"But they could still build something? They'd just have to do it so it didn't hurt the swamp."

"Right," Janice said sarcastically.

"Right," Ron said, watching her curiously. But he didn't ask any questions.

He didn't need to. Karen knew the moment of decision had come. "That's important," she said. "We need this new plant."

"What new plant?" Ron didn't sound angry or even surprised.

"The one they're going to build right up there." Karen pointed vaguely up the slope toward the flat rock.

"What kind of plant?" Janice sounded angry

"I don't know. They wouldn't tell us."

"But they're going to start it soon?" she snapped.

"In a month."

"A month," Janice groaned.

"So that map we did - that's what it was for?" Ron asked.

"I think so."

"They told us it was documentation for the sale of the land," Ron frowned. "So how do you know about it?"

"They needed to buy up our street, so they could build a road into the plant."

"Do you know where the road is going?" Ron seemed very interested now.

"Right down our street. From there it'll probably follow the path through the swamp."

"Can you show us?"

Karen took them back along the edge of the swamp to the path. "Right through there," she said, pointing. "It's the only place you can get across."

"They'd have to dump mountains of fill in there to build a road," Janice said angrily.

Ron looked right and left, carefully examining the swamp on either side of the path. "Let's walk it," he said. "I need to see this."

Karen led them along the path, a narrow ridge of high ground that fell away on both sides into swamp. Karen could easily see why the road would need to follow the path. On both sides, the soggy mud flats were dotted with shallow pools of water and clogged with damp and rotting vegetation. It was good for salamanders, but not so good for trucks.

They reached the other side of the swamp. "That's my house right up there," Karen said. "You can see the end of my street, too. The road will come down there and continue right on across the path."

Ron looked up at the dead end of Pond Street. His expression was grim. He spread his rain slicker at the base of a giant pine. "Let's sit down for a minute."

Karen and Janice sat with him on the slicker as a few heavy drops plopped near them in the pine needles.

"This is a problem, Karen – this road," Ron said, looking off into the swamp. "The water that feeds this swamp comes down from the mountains. This road would be at the upstream end of the swamp, so anything that came off the road would wind up in the water. That would be dangerous to our salamanders out there."

"It could wipe them out in no time," Janice added.

"Couldn't they build a fence to keep stuff from falling into the swamp?"

Ron shook his head. "The stuff that's dangerous would run right through a fence. It's stuff like salt in the winter, and the carbon sludge that diesels spew all year long."

"Isn't there some way to stop it from getting into the swamp?"

"It's possible," Ron said, thinking. "It depends on the amount of traffic and the location of the springs that feed the swamp. I don't know if they're going to want to do all the work to figure it out and do it right."

"You mean they might move the plant somewhere else?"

"They might. Developers don't like to deal with these environmental issues. It can hold them up for years."

"Oh, no," Karen said. "They want this done real soon."

"They always do," Janice said.

They were silent for a minute. Finally, Ron asked, "Is this plant a big deal for the town?"

"Very big," Karen nodded.

"That's what they always say," Janice snorted disdainfully.

"But it is," Karen protested. "Without the plant, the town might dry up and blow away. It's life or death for us."

"That's what it is for the salamanders, too," Ron said softly.

"I know."

"What should we do?" he asked, and it sounded like a real question to Karen. "Should we go to court and try to protect the swamp, or let the developers go ahead and build their road?"

Janice frowned at him as if the question was ridiculous.

Karen thought about it for a long time, even though she had known the answer for a week. "You've got to protect the swamp," she said. "The salamanders have lived here longer than we have. It's their home and they've got no place else to go."

Chapter 26: The Calm Before the Storm

Mrs. Taylor came home on Monday night and took a small white envelope out of her purse and handed it to Karen. Mrs. Taylor's name and address were typed on a corner of the envelope, but it hadn't come through the mail. There was no stamp.

Karen opened the flap and took out a check, also neatly typed, made out to Mrs. Elaine Taylor for $2,950.00 with a notation at the bottom, "deposit - #96 Pond Street." "Wow," she said.

"I know," her mother nodded. "Mr. Bellamy is handing out checks to everyone on the street. The closings are scheduled for the end of next month and construction will start right after that."

"Oh," Karen said, "That soon? What does it mean - 'deposit'?"

"That means it's part of the payment for the house. When we make the final sale, it gets deducted from the total that Mr. Bellamy owes us."

"If they don't build the plant here and Mr. Bellamy doesn't buy the house, do we have to give it back?"

"What? Oh, they're going to build the plant. I don't think there's much doubt now. They don't hand out money like this if they're not sure about it."

"Well, what if something came up? Would we still get to keep the money?"

Mrs. Taylor shrugged. "I think so, but don't worry. Nothing's going to come up."

"No," Karen said. "I hope not."

Just like Karen's mom, everyone on Pond Street thought it was a done deal. Mr. Bellamy gave out the checks and thanked them all for keeping the secret. He told them not to talk to anyone about it until construction started – just one more month. Finally, he announced that one of the local real estate agents was being brought in to help them find new homes. It would be done very quietly to avoid spreading rumors.

On another night that week, Karen's mom told her about a visit she'd had that day with Mrs. Torvald at the diner. Mrs. Torvald came in after the lunch rush had cleared and they sat down and had a cup of coffee together.

"Mrs. Torvald thinks you're pretty special," her mother told her.

"I like her too," Karen said.

"I didn't know you were friends with Davey."

"He's a nice kid," she said casually. "We talk sometimes."

Mrs. Taylor smiled. "That's good. I think he's a nice boy, too, from what little I know about him. And I'm really happy that you've found a new friend in the neighborhood."

Karen didn't have anything to say about that.

Fortunately, her mother changed the subject. "Mrs. Torvald particularly wanted to thank me for helping with Mr. Vandergaard. I didn't think she even knew about that."

"Um, I guess I told her something."

"Yes, that's what she said, and she was very grateful for it."

"I thought she needed to know as soon as possible."

"Is that why you ran off like that the other night?"

"Uh-huh."

169

"She said you have an amazing way of always knowing just the right thing to do."

"I don't know," Karen sighed. "I hope so."

"Well, I think so too, and I'm very proud of you."

Karen was silent again, so her mother went on. "She seemed a little surprised that I didn't know anything about your visit."

"I promised I wouldn't talk about it."

"Yes, she told me that too, and she was very impressed that you could keep a secret like that. She said you saw some things that might have been kind of disturbing."

"I guess."

"I think she felt very bad about that, and she told me to tell you that if you needed to talk to me about it, she wouldn't see that as breaking your promise."

"Oh."

"Do you want to talk to me about it?"

Karen thought about it for a long moment. "I don't think so. I think I'd rather forget about it."

Her mother paused for a moment, too. "Okay. I understand, but if you can't forget, then we should talk."

"Okay, Mom."

The week passed and nothing happened. Ron and Janice did not come back to the swamp, which left Karen to worry about the little baby salamanders alone. On that subject, there was no one to talk to, since it would lead right into the two scientists and their plan to protect the swamp, and that was something that worried her even more.

Davey came by a few times and they had fun together. He had stopped being weird, and Karen was starting to look forward to his visits. He never talked about the trouble with his father, the new plant, the salamanders, or any of that, and that was fine with Karen. She knew he didn't see it the same way she did. So long as it wasn't hurting his family, he didn't care what happened. Karen began to look forward to his visits, partly because it gave her a chance to stop thinking about all those other things, and partly, she had to admit, because she just liked him.

Mrs. Gunderson told her that the mayor had apologized profusely for Mr. Bellamy's rudeness and promised he would not bother her again. The old lady was thankful that she had been able to keep the whole incident from Mr. Gunderson, who was still weak but slowly recovering. Mrs. Gunderson asked Karen to keep coming by, hoping he'd soon be able to sit up long enough to read to. Karen kept hoping too, but mostly, she worried. Mr. Gunderson was old and sick, but Karen could not bring herself to think about the possibility that he might die. She needed him too much. The puzzle of the new plant was still unfolding, and she was in the middle of it. She didn't think she could face it without him.

Mrs. Taylor worked as hard as ever. She started talking to a real estate agent about places where she and Karen could live when their house was sold. During their few hours together, she quizzed Karen about what she wanted in their new house. Karen could think of only one thing. She wanted the woods and swamp just outside her back door. When Mrs. Taylor heard that, she shook her head sadly. The only houses in Pine Springs that had that feature were on Pond Street, and they would all be gone. Karen could see that her request had made her mother sad. She never brought it up again.

The school year was coming to an end, which should have filled Karen with excitement. Instead, she was filled with a feeling of dread, as if her whole world was about to fall apart, and it would be her fault when it did. She had no idea how Ron and Janice would go about protecting the swamp. She had no idea when Mr. Bellamy and the mayor would find out what they were doing. And she couldn't guess how she would hear about it when they did. Waiting for something to happen made her jumpy and irritable.

When her mother came home one night and told her that the closing on their house was scheduled for June 10, the Friday before her last week of school, Karen thought the legal efforts to protect the swamp must have failed. It gave her a feeling of relief that she knew was weak and selfish. The salamanders were still in the swamp, and the swamp was still in danger. She scolded herself for secretly wishing the whole problem would just go away, but it didn't matter what she wished. The problem would not go away.

Chapter 27: Roadblock

A few days later, her mother came home in the afternoon after one of her "short" days. Karen was doing her homework at the table, when her mother sank down on the chair across from her. Karen saw her bewildered expression and knew something was wrong.

"The mayor stopped by the diner this morning," Mrs. Taylor said. "He said the project ran into a roadblock, and he's having an emergency meeting tonight to tell everybody what's going on."

"What happened?" Karen asked, although she thought she knew the answer. "What kind of roadblock?"

"I don't know. The mayor wouldn't say, but he seemed very upset and angry about it."

"He did?"

"He said somebody must have leaked something about the new plant, or this never would have happened."

"Did he say who?" Karen asked, trembling.

"No. I don't think he knows, but I bet he'll find out."

"You think so?"

"Sure. Something as important as this – he'll probably get detectives from the State Police on it."

"Oh," Karen said in a small voice. Her mother didn't notice how pale she became.

"Isn't it a shame," Mrs. Gunderson said as they were driving to the meeting at Town Hall. "I guess these kinds of things happen, though."

"Yes, but I hope they don't give up on Pine Springs because of it," Mrs. Taylor said.

"I hope not, too." Mrs. Gunderson turned to Karen. "Mr. Gunderson said it doesn't matter what they do, Karen. You should still be proud of what you've done for all the people on this street."

"Who could have talked about this?" Karen's mother wondered. "Do they understand what they've done? Without that new plant, we might as well burn down the town and scatter to the four winds."

Karen was very quiet in the back seat.

At the meeting, the mayor looked grim. Mr. Bellamy looked grim. Mr. Wilson seemed upset. The people of Pond Street looked worried, and Karen was more worried than any of them.

Mayor Larson went up to the podium. It was odd to see him when he wasn't smiling. "I'm going to make this short," he said, "because I know you'll have a lot of questions. Yesterday, we were notified by the State Fish and Game Commission that no development could take place within half a mile of the swamp. As you all know, that's exactly where the new plant is supposed to be built. This news has caused Townsend Investment Trust to postpone the closings on your properties until this is all sorted out."

There was a loud response from the crowd. "They can't do that," someone yelled. "How's it any of their business?" someone else called out angrily.

"We're trying to get more information," the mayor continued, "but here's what we know so far: Evidently, some scientist discovered a new species of salamander living in that swamp. Since it's so new and rare, he went straight to the Friends of the Wilderness Club and got their lawyers to file for a temporary protective order on the swamp. The order was

174

issued, but it runs out in 60 days. By that time, they have to file a lot more information with the Commission, or the construction can proceed.

"Now you all know the company that's having Townsend build this plant wants it done in a hurry. This is going to cost them at least two months, maybe more. At this point, nobody can say if a plant can ever be built on that site. Mr. Bellamy just got back from meeting with the company, giving them the bad news. I'm going to let him tell you what they think about it. Jerry."

Mr. Bellamy came forward and looked out at the crowd. Like the mayor, he was not smiling. He seemed tired and angry, his face was puffy and sagging. "Our client is a major corporation," he said, "and this is a huge project for them. To have some slimy little lizard get in the way is ..." he searched for the word, "... unbelievable. When they heard about the injunction, they were ready to back out of the project right then and there."

"What?" someone gasped.

"No," several others yelled.

Mr. Bellamy sighed and raised his hands to silence them. "I talked them out of it – for now. We've got to see if this endangered species thing is for real and what kind of restrictions the Fish and Game Commission put on the proposed site. We've got our lawyers looking at all the documentation that's been brought forward so far, and it isn't much. There are some photographs, a genetic analysis, and the draft of a paper announcing the discovery. The lawyers tell me it's very unusual for a protective order – even a temporary one – to be written for a newly discovered species before the scientific community has even had a chance to study it and discuss it, a process that usually takes years. That hasn't happened in this case, so it's possible that this will turn out to be a false alarm, and the project will go ahead as planned, just delayed by a couple months.

"The thing that bothers me most about this, though, is the timing. If they had waited until they had all the scientific analysis in place before they filed for protection – the way this is normally done - we would have had construction well under way, and it would have been much harder, if not impossible for them to stop us. The only reason we can see that they filed so early on this one is that they knew we were about to start construction. And the only way they would have known that is if somebody told them."

This brought another angry buzz from the crowd.

"Of course, the leak could have come from anywhere, but if any of you have any knowledge of how this information got out, we'd like to hear from you."

Mr. Bellamy paused to let that sink in, and everyone began looking around the room suspiciously. Karen felt the blood rushing out of her head and her vision became clouded, but she had to look. She turned and saw Davey Torvald sitting with his parents two rows back on the other side of the aisle. He was staring at her with a tortured expression, and when their eyes met, Karen knew what she had to do

She timidly raised her hand.

Mr. Bellamy looked at her with an angry frown. "Yes, Karen?"

She stood up. "I know who told them about the project," she said softly.

Everyone looked at her, and there was perfect silence in the big room, as everyone strained to hear. "It was me."

"I know who told them about the project."

A loud angry buzzing broke out, like a nest of hornets. Mr. Bellamy stared, with his mouth half open. The mayor stood up and held his arms out, as if to quiet the crowd, but his expression was confused, uncertain.

"Karen, sit down," her mother whispered urgently.

But Karen knew it was too late for that, now. The words had been spoken and could not be taken back.

"Karen, why ..." the mayor faltered. "Why did you do that?"

The buzzing died so that everyone could hear Karen's soft reply. "The salamanders need protection. That's what the laws are for. Right?"

"Well, yes, but the plant is so important to this town, to all of us."

"They can still build it. They just have to make sure it doesn't hurt the swamp."

"But they might decide it isn't worth it. You heard what Jerry said. They might move the plant somewhere else."

"I know."

"You wouldn't want that," the mayor said, as if he'd proven some point.

"No, but I wouldn't want the plant to kill the salamanders either," Karen replied with just a trace of stubbornness.

The mayor shook his head, frowning. "That's not for you to decide."

"No," Karen said, frowning back. "I know that. It's for the laws to decide."

The mayor shook his head helplessly. "This isn't getting us anywhere," he said bitterly. "Jerry, would you tell everybody what happens from here."

The mayor sat down, and Karen did too. The crowd was too numb to protest.

Mr. Bellamy looked out at them. His face was set in an expression of anger and frustration. "Tomorrow our lawyers and engineers meet with the Wilderness Club. We're going to see if there is any way to move forward during the period of the injunction. We don't think there's much chance of that, but it could be helpful to find out where the most sensitive points of our plan are. The Club's people are going to do some more testing and surveying over the next few weeks, and all that will go into the final hearing in two months. We'll be keeping our client informed on all of this as we go along – and all of you, too, of course. We won't be able to reschedule the closings on any of your properties until we get the green light from everybody: the Wilderness Club, the Fish and Game Commission, our client, and the county. If that happens, we'll set up a new plan and get going again, but until then, we'll just have to wait and see.

"That's all I've got, for now," he sighed. "Any questions?"

The mayor came forward and stood beside Mr. Bellamy at the microphone. Several people stood up at once. The mayor pointed to Mr. McAllen, who stood tall and bony, with a sullen sneer on his face.

"What are you going to do about that child?" he said, pointing a long accusing finger at Karen, his voice harsh with anger. "She cost us a lot of money. Surely there must be some punishment for that."

Karen was shocked. This was the same stiff and silent old gentleman she went to church with every Sunday. Now he was leading the mob against her. They buzzed in agreement with his angry tone.

"Now, Mr. ..." the mayor started, trying to smooth things over.

Karen's mother jumped up. "What are you talking about, you stinking old hypocrite. If it wasn't for Karen, you wouldn't have had a chance at that money in the first place. Now sit down and shut up."

Mrs. Taylor glared at Mr. McAllen until he hesitantly sat down. The buzzing stopped and everyone looked at each other. Karen's mother looked defiantly around the room. When no one challenged her, she sat down and stared up at the stage. Karen slumped in her chair, looking at the floor, afraid to look up at the angry faces all around her.

The crowd was numbed by an overload of disappointment, anger, and frustration. How could this happen, they asked. What can we do? What are the odds the plant will be built in Pine Springs? Mr. Bellamy said that legal protection of endangered species often interfered with development. There was nothing the people of Pine Springs could do. It was all in the hands of the Townsend lawyers and technical people. He admitted that the alternate sites for the plant were far from Pine Springs. Townsend and their client intended to fight hard for the Pine Springs site, but there was a strong possibility that they would fail and the plant would be built at one of the alternate sites.

When the meeting was over, Karen felt as if she couldn't walk out with the crowd, but her mother would not wait. They got up and moved toward the door right along with everyone else. No one said anything to them. No one even looked at them. It was as if they were invisible behind a wall of silence.

In the car, Karen asked, "Did I do the right thing, Mom?"

Her mother helplessly shook her head and glanced at Karen in the rear-view mirror. "I don't know, Sweetheart. All I know is, it was too important a decision to make all by yourself. You should have talked with me about it."

"What would you have said to do?"

"I don't know. I guess I might have said to do nothing."

"That would have been threatening the salamanders with extinction."

Her mother was silent for a moment. "You thought about it a lot, didn't you?"

"Constantly, and the more I thought about it, the clearer it got. There were only two things I could do. I could either tell the scientists about the new plant or not tell them. If I told them, I knew they'd use the laws to protect the salamanders. Then I decided that that's what the laws are for - to decide if the salamanders should be protected, or not. So, if I didn't tell them, it would be almost like breaking the law. Wouldn't it?"

Her mother looked at her with a sad, perplexed look. "Who are these scientists?" she asked.

"Ron and Janice. They're nice, particularly Ron. It seemed like he was sorry about it. I think he could understand how important the plant was to all of us, but he also knew how important the swamp is to those salamanders. Anyway, he said you could build the plant so it wouldn't hurt the swamp, and it wouldn't even cost much money."

"I hope he's right."

"Me too," Karen agreed.

Chapter 28: Punishment

The school bus made only one stop on Pond Street. All the kids who lived on the street gathered at 7:15 in front of the McAllen's house to get on. Normally, Karen was one of the first at the stop. On the morning after her dramatic confession, she was one of the last.

She knew the kids would be talking about her and all the money she had cost their parents with her silly notion of protecting some salamanders down in the swamp. Even if they didn't understand what she had done, they would act out the anger they picked up from their parents. She just hoped they wouldn't beat her up. Karen dreaded having to face them, but she had no choice.

The usual talking, laughing and fooling around stopped as she approached. Some stared openly. Others looked away. Nobody said anything, but nobody attacked her, either. They stood apart from her and started whispering among themselves. Karen stood there, looking up the street to where the bus would appear. She knew they were talking about her, but she was determined to ignore them. She pretended she was as alone as she felt.

Davey was there, of course, standing with Matt Talbot, carefully not looking in her direction. Once, when she happened to glance at him, she caught his eyes on her. His expression was solemn and intense, as if he was staring into the glowing embers of a fire. That look cut through her like a knife. Suddenly, they were far apart. He quickly looked away.

Even though the bus came just a minute or two after Karen got to the stop, it seemed like a long wait. Karen was relieved to get on and move to her usual seat. No one sat beside her, but she often saw the Pond Street kids glancing at her as they talked with each other. The bus ride seemed to take a lot longer than usual.

School was better. Only the kids from Pond Street knew what she had done. The others treated her the same as always. She got through the day despite the sick feeling she got whenever she saw one of the Pond Street kids in the hall. She was glad there were only nine more days of school before summer vacation, but she wondered if the kids would forget by the next school year. This was the punishment that Mr. McAllen had wanted. Karen just hoped it wasn't a life sentence.

That afternoon, the ride home on the bus was just as bad as it was in the morning. When Karen got off the bus and walked down the hill, she realized that no one from Pond Street had said a single word to her all day. Karen was good at being alone. She had lots of practice, and it usually didn't bother her, but being deliberately shunned was different. She felt a stinging in her eyes and a swelling in her throat, but she blinked her eyes and took a deep breath, willing herself not to cry. She would not give them that satisfaction.

At home, she put her books away and went next door to report for work. She had not read to Mr. Gunderson in nearly two weeks, but she was praying that he would be up to it this time. Still, she was surprised when Mrs. Gunderson answered the door and showed her into the living room, where Mr. Gunderson was sitting in his usual chair.

Karen's joy at seeing the old man was quickly extinguished. He was wrapped in a blanket from his neck to his feet, even though it was quite warm. His sunken cheeks were shockingly pale, and his whole body was limp.

"Hal, Karen is here to read to you," Mrs. Gunderson said softly and left the room as Karen took her usual seat.

Mr. Gunderson smiled and moved his head vaguely toward the sound. "Hello, Karen," he said. His voice was weak and breathy. "I've missed our reading lately, but Mrs. Gunderson has told me what you've been up to."

"I've made a mess of things, haven't I?" Karen said sadly. "I wish I could have talked to you about it. I didn't know what to do."

"I don't know. I think you've been doing quite well on your own."

"Nobody else does," Karen sighed. "They all hate me."

"Do you think you did something wrong?"

"Not really, and nobody has even said I did, but it seems like they all wish I hadn't done it."

Mr. Gunderson laughed, a weak choking sound that seemed to hurt his chest. "I can believe that. Sometimes it's hard to do the right thing, and it doesn't always make you popular."

"It sure didn't this time. Nobody on the street will even speak to me."

"That must be very hard for you."

"It's horrible. I don't want everyone to be mad at me."

"Nobody does. It takes a special kind of courage to do the right thing when everybody wants you to do something else."

"But I don't even know if I did the right thing. Do you think I did?"

Mr. Gunderson thought for a moment. His tired and withered old face took on a soft, sad smile. "I do ... now. If you'd asked me before, I probably would have said don't do it. That's probably what the mayor wanted, wasn't it?"

"That's right."

"Mrs. Gunderson told me about the meeting last night. I probably would have told you to do nothing, to let it pass. That's why this project needed you, Karen. You're the only one who can see it. There isn't one of the adults involved in this project that would have done what you did, but there isn't one of them that can say you did anything wrong."

"But you know about this kind of business, Mr. Gunderson. You would have known what to do."

"You're right, I do know this business. I know it well enough to know that the business doesn't care about what's right and wrong. Business is measured in dollars and cents. It has no heart, no conscience. It's up to us, the people who do the business, to add that, and unfortunately, most of us have been at it too long. We've all been measured in dollars and cents so long we've forgotten there's any other way to measure what we do."

Mr. Gunderson's head dropped back against the cushion of the chair, and his eyes closed. He seemed very tired, so Karen let him rest for a minute, but he'd set so many ideas running around in her head, she finally had to ask him, "Does that mean business is bad?"

"No," he said, smiling sadly. "It's not bad, and it's not good. Business is just business. Only people can be good or bad."

"Were any of the people in this business bad?"

"Not really. But none of them were particularly good, either. That's why we needed you. When Mr. Bellamy tried to buy up the street for next to nothing, you said that wasn't fair. When we couldn't figure out how much the houses were worth, you pointed out that people live in them and those people have to go somewhere. When Mr. Bellamy wanted to leave the Torvalds out of the new deal because they'd already signed, you wouldn't let him. And then, when the project threatened to wipe out a whole species of salamanders, you said we should go by the law. If the law says they're more important than the new plant, then they should be protected. You've been the heart and conscience of this project right along the line. The rest of us weren't bad. We were just doing business. You were the only one doing good."

"But what do you think? Do you think the salamanders are more important than the new plant?"

"That's too hard a question for me. If you'd asked me two days ago, I would have said "no." Now, since I heard how you handled it, I'm inclined to agree with you. Many people have weighed that question to come up with the laws on it. I guess that's our best answer. Of course, you and I are probably the only two people in town who feel that way."

"I know, but what can I do? I feel like I've messed things up for everybody. There must be some way to make it all work out – I mean for everybody, including the salamanders."

Mr. Gunderson sighed and slumped a little lower in his chair. "I wish I could help you, but sometimes someone has to lose in order for someone else to win."

Silence fell over them as Karen thought about it. Mr. Gunderson couldn't see her sad frown turning defiant or her jaw tightening with determination, but he could hear it in her voice when she said, "That can't be right. There's got to be a way for us to live together. The salamanders aren't asking for much."

Chapter 29: No Way Out

The next day at school was even worse. The kids of Pond Street made it very clear they weren't going to talk to her, and there was no way for Karen to know how long that would last. It could be forever, she thought bitterly. But she refused to talk to them, too. She would not give them the opportunity to snub her.

What made it worse was that the other kids seemed to catch on. They might not know why they were doing it, but many of the kids from other parts of town started to avoid Karen, too. She couldn't find anyone to talk to at recess, and no one sat with her at lunch. It hurt so much, she didn't think she could stand it, but she wouldn't allow her pain to show. On the bus home, she held her head up and looked back at them with an expression that said, *I know what you're trying to do, but you can't hurt me. I'm not afraid.*

But that was a lie. She was afraid, and she was hurt. When she got home, she threw her books on the table, threw herself on the couch, and cried for 10 minutes straight. It helped to let out the pain that had been building insider her, but it didn't change anything. She sat up and saw that her tears had left a wet spot on the couch. She moved a pillow to cover it and went into the bedroom to change her clothes. There was homework to be done and the breakfast dishes were sitting in the sink, but all that would have to wait.

She tromped along the path through the swamp and looked down into the dark still waters of the ponds, wishing bitterly that those cute little salamanders had found somewhere else to make their home. When she reached the slope that marked the far side of the swamp, she turned toward the flat rock, where she planned to sit and think until she came up with something she could do to make it all work out. But before she got to the rock, she saw several people moving about down in the swamp.

"Karen," one of them yelled, waving.

It was Ron. Karen ran down the slope as eagerly as if he held the answer to all her problems.

"Hi," she said, coming up to Ron.

"I was hoping you'd show up," Ron said, grinning. "Guys, this is the famous Karen, who helped me find our little spotted friends here. Karen, these are some of my friends at the university."

There were three of them, two young men and a woman, all dressed for the swamp, with their jeans tucked into high rubber boots. They were scattered around one of the ponds, filling little tubes with water from the pond. They all looked up and waved to her.

Karen shyly waved back. "Where's Janice?" she asked.

"She had to meet with one of the professors on our paper," Ron said. "Anyway, this is my specialty, not hers."

"What are you doing?" Karen asked. "Are you looking for more of the baby salamanders?"

"No, we've got enough on them already. We've been out here the last few days doing a survey of the swamp and these hills. You know we went to the Fish and Game Commission to stop that development project you told me about – at least for awhile. Now we need to gather a lot more information to make sure whatever they do doesn't hurt the salamanders."

"I know. They told us about it when they stopped the project. Now everybody in town hates me for telling you about it." Karen tried not to let the pain of her isolation show, but there was a quiver in her voice that she could not control.

Ron frowned sympathetically. "How did they find out it was you that told me? I didn't say anything about you when we went to the Fish and Game Commission."

"I told them. I had to. I couldn't lie about it."

"So now everybody's going to blame you if the project doesn't go through, huh?"

"Yeah," was all Karen could say, struggling to hold back tears.

"Come on," Ron said. "Let's go talk this over. Maybe if we put our heads together we can come up with something."

Karen followed him up to the rock, where they sat down. It was a cool, breezy day. White puffy clouds kept passing across the sun, blocking out the bright warm sunshine, but the rock held the heat and kept them comfortable.

"A whole bunch of us met with the developers yesterday," Ron said. "Usually it's just the lawyers fighting it out in court, which doesn't do any good for anybody – except the lawyers. But these guys want to get something done, and they're smart enough to know they can't roll over us. You know why they're so eager to put the plant here?"

"No."

"For the water."

"What water? The water in the swamp?"

"Well, yes and no. They wouldn't take the water directly out of the swamp, but they want to use the same water that feeds it. There's a huge underground river that flows right below here. A small portion of that water bubbles up through springs down there in the swamp. The plant would drill down into the main river and get its water that way."

"Would that hurt the swamp?"

"Not at all. So long as they don't tap into the little tributaries that feed the springs, it wouldn't affect the swamp one bit."

"Really? Then can they go ahead and build it?"

"It's not that simple. There's a lot of other things involved in a plant this size. Do you know how big this thing is?"

"Not really, but it's big enough that the whole future of the town depends on it."

"I can imagine. Anyway, we talked about all kinds of things – waste water, runoff from the parking lots, airborne pollutants, truck traffic, anything that could possibly affect the swamp. We're lucky this is a fairly clean and modern operation they're talking about. We suggested some changes that would make it even safer for the swamp and they were very cooperative. The changes weren't very big or expensive, and they agreed to all of them except one."

"That's great." Karen was starting to get excited. Maybe there was a way out.

"It would be, except the one change they couldn't agree to is the most important one. Remember when you showed me where they planned to put the road through the swamp."

"Yeah," Karen said, "right from the end of my street."

"We can't let them do that. It's too dangerous to the swamp and to the salamanders. They're talking about four lanes of truck traffic, right through the middle of the swamp. They claim there's no other way to get from the plant to the interstate, and unfortunately, it looks like they're right. To go around the swamp to the south, they'd have to widen at least 10 miles of the old county road and then build another 15 miles of four lane roadway. To go around to the north, they'd have to cut the road through two or three miles of steep hillside. Neither way makes much sense."

"So what does that mean? What are they going to do?"

"I don't know. They said they'd look at it some more, but I don't think that's going to change anything. They might try to fight us on it, but I don't think they could win."

"You mean they might have to put the plant somewhere else?" Karen asked, unable to hide the disappointment in her voice.

"That's kind of what it looks like," Ron said gently. "That's bad news for the town, huh?"

"The worst." Karen was bitter. "And just as bad for me. If that plant doesn't get built because of me, I won't be able to live here anymore."

They were silent for a while. Then Ron said, "You really like this town, don't you?"

"Of course. I've never lived anywhere else. It's my home."

"Well then, there's one thing you might want to try. It's kind of a long shot, but it's the only way I can see to get that plant built here."

"What?" Karen demanded eagerly. "Tell me. I'll do anything."

Ron stood on the rock. "Look up there," he said, pointing to the rugged hills to the north.

Karen looked, but all she saw was a steep hillside covered in scrub pine. "Yeah?" she said uncertainly.

"We didn't do any surveying up there when we made the maps for your developer. The topographical maps from the state show nothing but steep hillsides. I don't think the developer has even looked up there to try to find a way around the swamp. Cutting their road into the slope of the hills is too expensive, but they don't even know if there might be some kind of natural shelf they could build on. I suggested it to them yesterday, but they didn't seem very interested. Maybe you could get them to check it out."

"Yeah," Karen said, thinking. "Maybe."

Chapter 30: Up on the Ridge

Ron had to go back down into the swamp to help his friends. Karen thought it was strange that he was gathering information to keep the plant out, while she was trying to figure out how to get it built. Well, business is strange. Science is strange. She wondered if she would ever understand either one, but she put those thoughts aside. There still might be an answer to this mess, and as always, it was up to her to find it.

She started tromping north, toward the hills. At first, she tromped over familiar ground. She had explored a lot of the scrub woods out beyond the swamp, but she'd only gone up to the head of the swamp once or twice. It was almost four o'clock, and she knew she had to be home by seven to get her homework done and the dishes washed before her mother got home. Hope kept her moving over rough ground, through patches of thick brush and around jutting rocks. In an hour, she made it to the head of the swamp. She was tired and scratched and dirty, but nothing was going to slow her down. She figured she had an hour to look for a flat passage around the swamp before she had to turn back.

It didn't look promising. The hills were like a wall, rising steeply from the gently rolling terrain she'd just traversed. The only way to put a road around the head of the swamp would be to blast it out of the hillside – exactly what Townsend didn't want to do. Karen could see that the steep slope ran right down into the swamp. She walked along the base of the slope, looking for what Ron had described - a flat shelf along the hillside where a road could go. There was nothing like that. After an hour, she had to turn back and hurry home.

Karen was just finishing the dishes when her mother got home. She knew right away from her mother's somber face that something was wrong.

"Somebody leaked the news about the plant all over town," she said, as she dropped her purse on the little side table by the door.

"That's great," said Karen sarcastically, hanging the dish towel in its usual place on the handle of the oven. "They probably know all about what I did too."

"I'm afraid so. They're all talking about it. I got an earful and it made me so mad, I had to give it back to a couple of them." Mrs. Taylor laughed bitterly. "I think I lost a few tips today."

"Just ignore them, Mom. I'm getting used to it already. The kids have been giving me the silent treatment for two days. We've got to hold our heads up. We didn't do anything wrong – especially not you."

"I know, Sweetheart, but that doesn't mean we won't get punished for it. It's so unfair."

"Don't worry," Karen said with surprising confidence. "We'll get through it."

"I hope so. But they better figure out a way to get that plant built or we'll have to get out of town."

"We'll figure it out."

But Karen's confidence slipped away over the next week.

First there was Eva's message on Saturday morning. Karen had come to the library as usual, with a thousand things to write about. Since she had no one else to talk to, Eva was going to have to listen to all her troubles. She figured she might be there for an extra hour, even. But it didn't turn out that way. The first thing she did was read the message from Eva, which was waiting for her. It only took a minute.

> Karen, what did you do? My father said you cost us a lot of money and you killed the whole town. Now I can't write to you anymore. He won't let me. So this email is just to tell you that and to tell you not to write to me either. If my Dad sees any messages from you, I'll get in trouble. He's really mad. They won't get me a puppy, now, because of this money thing. Goodbye, Eva

School was terrible. She had to walk through the halls and sit in class with invisible walls around her. At the meeting, those walls had protected her, but now they were like a prison. No one came near, and no one talked to her. Karen maintained a calm, expressionless face and did not try to break through their cage of silence. She buried the hurt deep inside her, but it was still there, just waiting to bubble up unexpectedly to sting her eyes and swell her throat. Strangely, it hurt most when she ran into Davey on the bus, or in the halls, or on the playground. She would see that intense blank stare of his for just an instant before he turned away. For some reason, that bothered her more than any of the rest of it. She had lied to her mother. She wasn't getting used to it, and she was starting to realize that she never would.

Mr. Gunderson was too sick for reading, and Karen missed him. She didn't think he could actually help her, but talking to him always made her feel better. He understood what she had done. He even admired her for it. Just hearing his voice would have been a comfort.

Even her mother was distant, though for completely different reasons. Her joke about losing tips was no joke. She was working harder than ever and not making enough for them to get by. Karen thought her mother was worried about the money and their social isolation, just like she was, but there was something else.

One night, when they were sitting at the table, her mother asked her, "Karen, do you think I'm being selfish?"

"What?" Karen was shocked. "No. Of course not. What do you mean?"

"Mr. Bellamy came into the diner today. He was furious with you, and he said I was a bad mother. He said he could make it hard for us in this town." Her mother's face was hard with anger. "That stuff didn't bother me. He's just a jerk, but he did say one thing that might be true."

"What?"

"He said you needed a father."

Karen was silent for a moment. "That's none of his business," she finally said softly.

"No, but that doesn't mean it's not true."

"Well, it's not." Karen suddenly felt all the loneliness and uncertainty rise like a lump in her throat, but she tried to be defiant. "We do okay, Mom. We don't need anybody else."

"Is that how you really feel?" her mother asked gently. "It seems like every time I push you to go out and find new friends, you bring up the fact that I haven't gone on any dates. Maybe you're right. Maybe I should be thinking about finding you a new father."

"No, Mom. I'm okay. I know nobody could ever replace Dad. I don't ... I don't want ..." But she couldn't think of what to say anymore. Thoughts and emotions were too jumbled inside her to come out in words.

Her mother came around the table and put an arm across her shoulder. "It's alright, Sweetheart. You're right. We do have each other, and that's a lot. Maybe we just need to remind ourselves sometimes it's not a bad thing to let other people into our lives, too."

"I know." Karen turned to her and hugged her. "But now I've ruined all that. Nobody will come near us anymore."

"You didn't ruin anything, Darling. You've done some wonderful things, and someday they'll see that."

Despite her mother's comforting words, Karen had little hope that the town would ever forgive her. Grimly, she doubled her efforts to find a solution. There had to be an alternative to Pond Street for the access road to the new plant. She went out to the hills at the head of the swamp and searched for the magic passage every chance she got.

She walked back and forth along the base of the slope that rose almost like a cliff up to the ridge. She saw no place where a road could be built into the hillside. After going over the same ground for the third or fourth time, she was almost ready to give up, when another idea struck her. What if she climbed the steep slope and searched for a possible roadway from above? Maybe the terrain would reveal something she had missed from below. It was worth a try.

She picked a spot about a quarter of a mile from the head of the swamp, where broken rocks formed small ledges that offered a way to zig-zag up the slope without having to grab onto the scrub trees and brush to pull herself up. It was still a hard and treacherous climb. Several times she had to turn back to find a way around a rock wall that blocked her. It took her almost a half hour to climb a hundred feet from the base. She was hot, tired, and bleeding from where she'd scraped her knee after slipping on some loose rocks.

Her head was down, watching where she placed her feet, when she suddenly came upon a wide flat space. It had been perfectly invisible from below, masked by the thick cover of trees and the steep slope. She was so surprised that she looked around for a moment before realizing that this was exactly what she'd been looking for. The ledge ran off as far as she could see to the left and right. If it went far enough to the left, it might be a way around the swamp.

The sun was sinking and she had to get home. It would be a dangerous descent if she got stuck up there in the dark, but she had to find out if this was really the answer she'd been searching for. She set off to the left and found it much easier going than the climb had been. It was level and covered with mature pines that left her path relatively free of brush. Most of it was 30 to 40 feet wide. In ten minutes, she stood looking down at the head of the swamp.

The sun was low over the mountains, turning the swamp into a big dark shadow. To the left of the swamp, she could see where the plant was supposed to be built. She tried to envision a wide roadway descending the hillside to the proposed site from where she stood. It was hard to imagine, but what did she know about building roads? On the other side of the swamp, she could vaguely see Pond Street running up out of the shadows toward the interstate that curved around the town. More importantly, Karen thought she could follow the vague dent in the tree cover that was the only indication of the shelf she had found. It seemed to curve around the swamp and descend gradually toward the town. It looked as if she could follow it almost back to where Pond Street met the old county highway. She decided to try to make her way home that way and set off with a lightness to her step that was as much from the excitement of her discovery as it was from the need to beat the darkness.

Karen walked down Pond Street as the last twilight faded from the sky. She was a mess and her homework was waiting, but her most pressing need was for food. She went straight to the refrigerator and started fixing a sandwich.

She was just about to sit down at the table to eat, when her mother walked in.

"Hi Mom," Karen greeted her, grinning.

Her mother looked at her with surprise turning instantly to concern. "Karen! What happened to you?"

"Oh, this?" Karen looked down at her torn and bloodied jeans, her dusty boots and she knew she looked a mess. "I was just out tromping through the woods. I guess I slipped."

"You sure you didn't get into a fight at school?"

"Of course not. I was ..."

"Are you just having dinner now?"

"Um, yeah."

"So you were out in the woods all afternoon?"

"Yeah, and I found ..."

"What about your homework?"

"I'll do it. I was just going to eat something first and get cleaned up."

"Okay, but you better step on it. It's getting late."

"I know."

Karen sat down and started eating her sandwich. She could see that her mother wasn't listening to her, and she knew there was something on her mind. Karen had been bursting with the news of her discovery, but finding her mother so preoccupied made her pause. She didn't know if they could actually build a road on that odd flat shelf she had found. She decided not to tell anyone about it until she could get the mayor or someone who knew about roads to look at it and tell her if it would work. There was no sense in getting everybody excited for nothing.

Mrs. Taylor was washing her hands at the kitchen sink. Over her shoulder she said, "The mayor called a town-wide meeting for tomorrow night. I'm sure it's about the plant. The whole town was buzzing about it today. Some people are saying they must've okayed it. Others think he's going to announce that it's off. I don't know if I even want to go. What do you think?"

"We've got to go," Karen said with certainty. "I don't care how many dirty looks we get, we've got to be there."

"Well, okay, but it's not going to be fun." Mrs. Taylor sounded fearful but resigned.

"We'll see," Karen said softly.

Chapter 31: A Little Help from Her Friends

The next day at school was torture. This time, it wasn't the kids' silence that got to Karen. She didn't even notice it. All she could think of was what she would do when the bell finally rang for the end of the day. But each lesson seemed to drag on and on. As much as she tried to pay attention, Karen couldn't keep her mind on what her teacher was talking about for two minutes at a time. She had much more important things to think about. Every time she looked up at the clock, it seemed like the minute hand was stuck right where it had been the last time she looked.

Finally, the bell rang and the school day was over. With her books tucked under her arm, Karen flew out the door. Running all the way to Town Hall, it seemed like her feet never touched the ground. She burst into the mayor's office panting with excitement.

Mrs. Pettibone looked up from her typing and her eyes were wide behind the funny glasses. "Goodness!" she exclaimed.

Karen stood at the rail, barely restraining herself from jumping up and down. "Where's the mayor. I've got to see the mayor."

"Oh, my dear, you can't ... Wait, aren't you that Taylor girl, the one who caused all this trouble?"

"Yes, but I ..."

"I really don't think the mayor would wish to see you," Mrs. Pettibone said coldly.

"But I ..."

"In any case, he's busy preparing for tonight's town meeting. He will not be seeing anyone this afternoon."

"But it's very important. I have to talk to him before ..."

"That's impossible," Mrs. Pettibone snapped, "and I can't think what you could possibly have to say to him after what you've done."

"But I can fix it."

"No you can't. Mayor Larson left strict instructions that he was not to be disturbed, and I certainly do not intend to disobey him for any of your foolishness. Now, will you please leave this office."

"But ..."

Mrs. Pettibone rose from her chair. Her face was red with anger and her eyes had narrowed to slits. She pointed to the door. "Now. Go."

"But can I talk to Mr. Bellamy? Do you know where he is?"

"He's with the mayor." She continued to point to the door. "Do I have to call security?"

Karen sighed. She turned toward the door. "But they ..."

"No," Mrs. Pettibone almost shouted. "Go."

Karen went out the door and stood in the hall, blinking back tears. She couldn't think what to do. She had the answer – maybe – but no one would listen. With no other place to go, her feet trudged slowly home.

She had just started down Pond Street, when she saw Davey Torvald zoom down his driveway on his bike. He didn't see her until he had started pedaling up the street toward her. When he did see her, he didn't seem to know what to do. He stopped pedaling for a moment and swerved, as if he was going to turn around, but he didn't. He steered his bike over to the far side of the street and looked away, as if he didn't even see her.

"Davey," Karen yelled. "Stop. I want to talk to you."

Davey kept pedaling, but he looked at her. "No," he said angrily. "I can't." He turned away and rode past her, his face screwed up in a fierce scowl.

Karen stopped at the Gundersons' place and hopelessly knocked at the door.

It took some time for Mrs. Gunderson to come to the door. She shook her head sadly. "No, dear, not today."

"But will he be at the meeting tonight?"

Mrs. Gunderson looked worried. "Shh," she whispered. "I don't want him to even know about that meeting. He'd be just fool enough to try to go. He's not well. Please tell your mother I won't be going either."

She shut the door and Karen walked across the lawn, dejected and bewildered. For once, she had no idea what to do. In the house, she went to the table and picked up a note that said, "Had to run an errand for Mr. Colston. Pick you up around 5:00 to go to the meeting. Love, Mom."

Karen looked at the clock – 3:10. She dropped her book bag and flopped on the couch, staring up at the ceiling and trying to think. Nothing came into her head. There was nothing she could do. After a few minutes of that, she got up and put on her jeans and boots. She went down the path to the swamp, where she wandered aimlessly among the pools, picking her way around the soggy spots until she came to a fallen tree. There she sat, in the cool damp shade, trying only to forget the awful situation she'd gotten herself into.

She had almost succeeded when one of the yellow and pink spotted salamanders appeared on a little mound of dead leaves that rose just out of the water near the shore of the pond. The salamander was perfectly still, and so was Karen. She watched him, scarcely blinking for almost a full minute. The little black eyes seemed to look past her.

"Well, Newton," Karen said softly, "I hope you appreciate what I've done for you. It looks like you get to keep your home, but I lose mine."

The salamander's head turned toward the sound of her voice, but otherwise, he didn't move.

"Everybody hates me," Karen continued. "It doesn't seem fair, but I guess that's the way this business works."

The salamander stayed perfectly still.

"Sometimes I wish I was more like you, so I could just swim away and disappear into the mud when trouble comes around."

She stumbled slightly when she slid down off the log. When she looked up, she expected the salamander to be gone, but he was right where he had been, not more than ten feet away. The black eyes looked like tiny beads stuck on his head. They still seemed fixed on her, although it was really impossible to tell where they were looking. Karen was fascinated. She moved slowly toward him, speaking in gentle even tones.

"Maybe everything will work out. Is that what you're saying? Are you sticking around to wish me luck?"

She was standing right over the salamander, looking down at him with a soft smile. The little head suddenly bobbed up, as if to look at her face, but again the salamander stayed where it was. Karen bent down and slowly reached her hand out, leaving it resting on the leaves just an inch from the creature's head. Still he didn't move.

"You're a brave one, aren't you?"

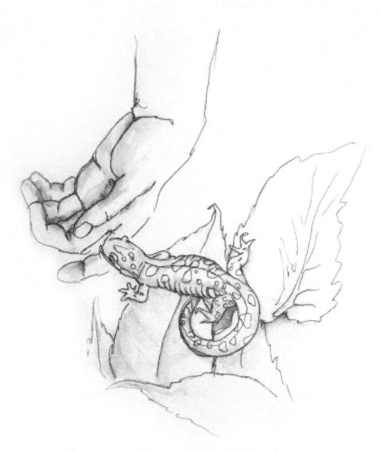

"Are you sticking around to wish me luck?"

The salamander took two quick steps forward and put its front feet on her finger. It stood there like that for only a second or two then vanished in a wriggling dive. Karen stood up and laughed out loud. She ran home, washed up, and put on her good dress. She was ready for the meeting.

Chapter 32: Wait!

Karen's mother was late. It was almost 5:30 when she pulled into the driveway. Karen ran out and jumped in the car.

"Mom, where have you been?" she complained. "The meeting's probably starting right now."

"I know. I had to go down to the city to pick up some things for Mr. Colston. I got stuck in traffic coming back. I don't know why you're so eager to get there, anyhow. If this is bad news, everybody in town is going to want to roast us over a slow fire."

"I know, Mom. I told you a million times – that's why we've got to be there. We've got to show them we've got nothing to be ashamed of."

They rushed to the high school and into the gym. Karen was relieved that the people on the stage were still in their seats. The meeting hadn't started. But when she looked around for seats, she saw that the bleachers and all the chairs out on the basketball court were full.

"Over there," her mother said, pointing.

Karen followed her and started edging into one of the rows of seats on the court. Suddenly she saw the two empty seats her mother was heading for. Right next to those two seats sat Mr. and Mrs. Torvald and Davey. The seat her mother intended for Karen was right next to Davey Torvald. Karen felt like she might faint, but there was nothing she could do. The Torvalds stood up to let them pass, but Karen didn't have enough courage to look up to see the angry expression she knew she'd find on Mr. Torvald's face. She sat down next to Davey, but she didn't look at him or say a word. She folded her hands in her lap and kept her eyes down until Mayor Larson went up to the microphone.

"Good evening, everyone," he said. "We're here tonight to address an issue of great importance to all of us here in Pine Springs. We all know how much we depend on the factory for our bread and butter, and we've seen what the cutbacks there have been doing to our town. As your mayor, I've been working with many of the civic and business leaders here to try to address this problem. Over the last several months, we've been exploring a particular opportunity very seriously. I know many of you have heard something about it. In fact, from some of the questions that have made their way to my desk, it seems the rumor mill has been running wild. I called this meeting to set the record straight, and to put this project into perspective as a part of our ongoing business development program."

The mayor sounded like he was going into one of his long boring speeches. Karen wasn't paying much attention. She was looking at the other people sitting behind him on the stage. One of them was Mr. Bellamy, but she didn't think she knew the others until she looked a little closer. One of them was Ron, the scientist who had discovered the pink and yellow spotted salamanders. He looked so different in a suit and tie that she hadn't recognized him at first. Karen was surprised to see him and immediately began to wonder why he was there.

The mayor was going on with lots of big words that Karen tuned out, but he finally came to the point. "... unfortunately came up against an unexpected roadblock, which has led us to conclude that this project will not be going forward."

The crowd groaned and broke into a hostile chatter that included a few angry shouts.

The mayor held up his hands. "I know, I know. You're disappointed. So am I. This project would have been great for our community, and we worked tirelessly for many months to make it happen. In the end, we ran up against a problem that could not be overcome. But what I want you to understand is that this is not unusual. The developer on this project tells me that only one out of every four or five proposals ever gets built. We have several other projects under consideration, and we're confident that one of them will go through to completion. Of course, since these projects involve important competitive information, they must be kept confidential. We would not be discussing this one, if word of it had not leaked out. But since it did, and the rumors are running out of control, I thought we should all hear the real story. So, I've asked some of the key people involved in the project to give you the facts. First, we'll hear from Jerry Bellamy, representing the developer, Townsend Investment Trust. He's worked with us from the beginning on this one. Jerry."

Mr. Bellamy got up and explained the project. For the first time, Karen learned that the new plant was being developed for the Dew Drop Corporation, a major bottler of juice and soft drinks. They had asked Townsend to find a site with three important characteristics: 1) plentiful water, 2) a skilled and enthusiastic workforce, and 3) ready access to the interstate. Pine Springs was perfect. It had an endless supply of extremely pure mountain water flowing underground, workers displaced by the diminishing business of the factory, and ramps to the interstate less than a mile from the proposed site. He put up a slide that showed a map of the new plant and the interstate. The swamp was a big green blotch sitting right between them. The proposed access road running down Pond Street and over the path through the swamp was outlined in red.

Mr. Bellamy pointed to the swamp. "Unfortunately, we aren't the only ones who like that good clean mountain water. It turns out there's a little spotted salamander that lives in that swamp and nowhere else in the world. When we discovered that, we started talking to the Fish and Game Commission and the Friends of the Wilderness to see if any of our plans might harm the salamanders. It turned out that the road we planned to build right here -" he pointed to the double red lines, "the critical access to the interstate – had a high risk of damaging the fragile balance of the swamp and threatening this rare species. That was a risk that none of us were willing to take. My company has a strict policy prohibiting work on any project that would have a negative environmental impact. The Dew Drop Corporation is strongly committed to environmental protection. And your mayor has also been quite clear on this. In the end, we all agreed. Since we could not build the road without endangering the salamanders, the project had to be cancelled."

Karen was confused. She was relieved they weren't publicly blaming her for shutting down the project, but the story they were telling wasn't right. Mr. Bellamy and the mayor had never been the least bit worried about the salamanders. She was sure they would have built the road right through the swamp if Ron and the Friends of the Wilderness hadn't gone to court. Why was Mr. Bellamy lying, and why was Ron letting him get away with it?

A frustrated mutter rose from the crowd as Mr. Bellamy went back to his seat and the mayor came forward. "Now I know you've all got questions, so I've asked some of the key people to help me answer them." He pointed to the other men seated behind him. "Beside Mr. Bellamy is Mr. Donald Cross, CEO of the Dew Drop Corporation. Next is Mr. William

Burke of the Friends of the Wilderness. And finally, Mr. Ron Walker, who discovered this new species of salamander living in our back yard.

"Before I open the floor to questions, I want you to remember that this project is just one of several we've been working on. The fact that we couldn't bring it to completion is disappointing, but it's not the end of the world. We may have to go down a few more dead ends before we find the one that will get us to the bright future we all want for Pine Springs. Now, questions ..."

Dozens of hands went up in the crowd, and Karen's was one of them. Some of the question were angry. Some were just confused. The mayor would not talk about any of the other projects, but every other question was answered in great detail. Ron even had to get up and explain what was so special about the salamanders. He said that every species is important to the balance of nature that we all depend on, but that these salamanders could also prove to be very valuable to scientific research. This species evolved after being isolated in the swamp tens of thousands of years ago. The opportunity to study their adaptation to the environment of the swamp was potentially very important to science. The crowd did not seem very interested in the balance of nature or scientific research, but Karen saw the gentle smile in Ron's eyes and she was proud that she had helped him.

After about a dozen questions and a dozen long answers, the crowd seemed to reluctantly accept the fact that the new plant was not going to be built. They were ready to go back to their weary struggles without the bright new possibilities they had so desperately hoped for. Disappointment weighed heavily on them, but they were used to it. Karen felt like she was the only one in the whole gym who hadn't given up.

After each question was answered, she frantically waved her hand in the air, but the mayor just didn't seem to see her.

"All right," he said. "I guess that's about all we've got time for tonight. I think you got a good understanding of what happened. I know it's not good news, but the next time we get together like this, I hope we'll be talking about a new project that will bring us the jobs and economic opportunities that we all want for Pine Springs. Thank you and good night."

Karen stood up on her chair and shouted, "Wait!"

Everybody turned to look at her, most with surprise, but some with anger distorting their faces. Her mother said, "Karen!" Davey whispered, "What are you doing?" but there was no anger in his voice, only wonder. The mayor's face was one of the angry ones.

"What, Karen?" he demanded, frowning.

Still standing on the chair, Karen looked out at the sea of faces and took a deep breath. She was terrified, but she couldn't back down now. This was her last chance to make it all work out.

"I just wondered if you checked for other places to build the access road." Her voice was shaky, but loud enough for everyone to hear.

"Of course we did," the mayor snapped.

"Did you see the wide flat shelf that goes around the head of the swamp about a hundred feet up the hillside?"

"I … I'm sure …" He put his hand over the microphone and turned to Mr. Bellamy, who frowned and shook his head. The mayor turned back to the microphone. "Karen, the decision is made. We did everything we could. Don't …"

"Wait a minute," another voice came from the crowd. It was Mr. Vandergaard who got slowly to his feet. "She's right. That's the old logging road. I completely forgot about it.

212

That cut was done sixty years ago. It used to go right around the edge of town to the mill, but it got cut off when they put the interstate through. As I recall it was plenty wide for your access road."

The mayor opened his mouth to reply, but then decided he needed more information. He went back to the others seated on the stage and they talked together in whispers, while the audience began an excited chatter. Mr. Bellamy looked upset. He kept shaking his head and frowning. The mayor looked confused. Ron was trying not to smile, but he wasn't doing a very good job of it. Finally, the man from the Dew Drop Corporation, Mr. Cross, came up to the microphone.

"Young lady," he said, "maybe we didn't look hard enough. If we can put a road up there, I still want to build in Pine Springs. Would you take us out there tomorrow, so we can take a look at it?"

"I'd love to," Karen said.

The crowd was so stunned by this sudden turnaround, there was perfect silence for about five seconds. Then there was a loud cheer from somewhere in the bleachers and the whole crowd joined in, cheering and clapping wildly.

Karen climbed down off her chair and her mother hugged her. Everyone crowded around trying to pat her on the back and tell her how much they loved her. But the best part for Karen was when they were all filing out of the gym. Davey caught her arm and whispered, "You're amazing."

Chapter 33: The Road Home

The mayor told Karen they would meet at 9:30 the next morning at her house for the expedition to the hillside. He tried to keep it quiet, but somehow word leaked out. When the mayor's party got to Karen's house, half the residents of Pine Springs had crowded onto Pond Street. The mayor talked to Ron, then got up on Karen's front step and announced that the crowd could not go with them through the swamp. He told them to go home and promised to hold another meeting at noon in the high school gym to tell everybody what they found.

Then Karen took them through her backyard and out onto the path through the swamp. The party included Karen, the mayor, Mr. Bellamy, Mr. Cross, Ron, Mr. Burke, and another man that Mr. Cross introduced to Karen as Mr. Carson, an expert on road building. Only Ron and Karen were dressed for hiking. The rest of the men wore light colored khaki pants and sneakers. The mayor wore low canvas sneakers with a thin flat sole, the kind they call boat shoes. Karen hoped he wouldn't break an ankle. She tromped along the familiar path in the lead, with Mayor Larson and Mr. Cross at her side. When they were right in the middle of the swamp, Mr. Cross stopped and looked around at the giant trees with their majestic limbs hanging gracefully over still dark pools.

"Karen," he said with a kind of awe, "this is so beautiful. Were we really going to put a four lane road through here?"

"That was the plan."

He shook his head sadly. "That would have been a shame even if there weren't a rare salamander down there."

Karen followed his gaze down into the familiar swamp. "I think so, too," she said, with a pang of guilt. She had tried to help the mayor and Mr. Bellamy make that plan come true.

"That's the problem with maps," Mr. Cross said. "Something like that seems to make sense when it's just a bunch of lines on a piece of paper."

"That's for sure," Karen smiled.

"Now show me what else we missed by looking at maps," Mr. Cross said.

"Come on," Karen said, running ahead eagerly.

When they came to the far side of the swamp, Mr. Cross stopped again and asked Mr. Bellamy where the plant would sit. He seemed a little angry with Mr. Bellamy, who acted kind of embarrassed, almost afraid of him. Mr. Bellamy pointed out into the scrub. Mr. Cross nodded and they turned toward the steep hills to the north.

There was no path. Karen had to pick her way through the brush, over rough and rocky ground. Mr. Bellamy and Mayor Larson had some problems with the scratchy bushes and uneven footing. They were soon sweating and dropping behind. Karen hid a smile and slowed down to let them catch up.

When they reached the base of the slope that seemed to rise suddenly straight up to the ridge, Mr. Bellamy was out of breath and angry. "Well," he said, "where is it? Where is this magic pass? It'd cost a fortune to put a road into the face of this cliff."

"It's right up there," Karen said. "You can't see it from here because of the trees."

"Show me," said Mr. Cross.

Karen grinned and started up the steep slope. Mr. Cross, Mr. Carson, Ron and Mr. Burke all followed. The mayor and

Mr. Bellamy hesitated, then looked at each other and started to climb after the others. Karen was so excited, she practically skipped from rock to rock like a mountain goat. She was far ahead of the others when she came out on the flat shelf. It was even wider than she remembered. She laughed and twirled around on the soft pine needle carpet. Suddenly Ron's head poked up over a rock. He looked around in amazement.

"You found it," he said.

"Right where you said it would be," Karen answered.

"I was just guessing."

"Do you think they can build the road here?"

Ron shrugged. "I've got no idea."

Mr. Cross came up to them, slightly out of breath. He put his hands on his knees and rested for a moment. Then he too looked around at the wide flat shelf. "Wow," he said. "Now I see what you were talking about."

"Can you build a road on it?"

"I'm sure," Mr. Cross nodded seriously. "The question is can we build a road down from here. That's a pretty steep slope."

"There must be a way," Karen said desperately. "This flat shelf goes right around the swamp and almost connects with the old county road right near the ramps to the highway."

"I don't know," Mr. Cross said. "It sounds good. If Mr. Carson can make it up here, we'll ask him."

They didn't have to wait long. Mr. Carson had stopped to pick up samples of soil and rock from the hillside. He came up onto the shelf and looked around. "Well," he said, appreciatively.

"What do you think, Fred," Mr. Cross said. "Karen and a whole town are waiting for your word on pins and needles."

"This is perfect – stable, flat. No problem." He turned to Karen. "You say this goes all the way around the swamp, wide and flat like this?"

"Yes. And it's a gentle slope down on the other side." Karen frowned. "I just don't know about getting down on this side."

Mr. Carson turned to scan the hillside as it curved gently toward the south. "Yeah. That's going to be tricky," he said thoughtfully. Then he brightened. "But it sounds like we've got two thirds of the problem licked. Maybe we can resort to a little engineering magic for the rest."

Mayor Larson, Mr. Burke, and Mr. Bellamy straggled up to them. Mr. Bellamy was very red in the face and his shirt was stained with sweat. He dropped to the ground at the foot of a pine tree and rested against the trunk, panting and glancing reproachfully at Karen, as if she was the cause of his exhaustion. Mayor Larson was red and puffing, too, but he looked around eagerly. This was what he had come for.

"Look at this," he gasped. "You can build ... a road here," he said to Mr. Cross.

"Yes we can," Mr. Cross agreed. "But can we build a road from here," and he pointed to the pine needle carpet on which they stood, "down to there?" He pointed to the base of the steep slope.

"Oh, right," the mayor said. "How do we find out about that?"

"Let's see what's a little further on. They probably used this road for working the hillside, but they logged off all that flat area down there, too. I'll bet they took the timber out this way. They must have found a place where the trucks could get up and down."

Mr. Bellamy wasn't very eager to go on, but he raised himself painfully from the ground and trudged with the rest of them as they set off. Mr. Carson walked near the edge of the old road, which had been overrun by the regrowth of the pine forest. He seemed to be surveying the hillside for any natural formation where a road could descend.

Karen estimated that they had gone nearly a mile, when Mr. Carson suddenly stopped and pointed. "There," he said.

The whole party rushed to his side, looking eagerly in the direction he had indicated. About a hundred yards ahead, they saw a narrow canyon cut into the hillside. Karen didn't think it looked very promising for a road. It looked like a piece of the hillside had simply collapsed and slid out onto the scrub flats, leaving a gouge in the hillside that was filled with jagged boulders and tangled brush. It seemed to be more of a barrier than a potential roadbed, but the more she studied it, the more she understood what Mr. Carson was seeing. If you ignored the broken rock, you could see that the basic shape of the rockfall was a gentle slope down to the flats.

"What?" the mayor asked. "You think you can put a road down through that?"

"I can put a road anywhere, if you give me enough money," Mr. Carson laughed. "The question here is how much?"

They continued on and found that the wide shelf the loggers had cut into the hillside continued into the canyon, descending sharply to the floor, where it was lost in heavy brush.

"Alright," Mr. Carson announced, "this is it. We don't need to go any farther today. Karen, if we walk back along this old logging road, will it get us back to your house?"

"It sure will. I've done it, but I had to cut through a patch of sticker bushes to get out to the old highway." She glanced at Mr. Bellamy's red and scowling face. "Maybe some of you would rather go back the way we came. It's a little easier."

Mr. Carson looked around at the others. "Well, I don't know about the rest of you, but I've got to see the other end."

Mr. Cross immediately said, "Me too."

"I'll take my chances with the sticker bushes," the mayor said.

They all agreed to go back by way of the old logging road, though Mr. Bellamy didn't seem very happy about it. They walked comfortably in the shade of the pines that grew up right out of the abandoned road. Karen was surprised how quickly they came to the head of the swamp. It couldn't have been more than a mile. Standing above the swamp, they looked down into its dark green tangle, where, here and there, small pools reflected the sunlight like little sparkling jewels.

From there, the track of the road sloped gradually toward town and became clogged with underbrush. Soon, they could hear the faint whoosh of traffic on the interstate. That's when they hit the thicket of sticker bushes Karen had warned them about.

Karen knew how to carefully pick her way through, but some of the men managed to get themselves so wrapped up in the thorny vines, she had to help them get unstuck. It ended up taking almost half an hour to get through the thicket, even though it was only about twenty yards deep. They finally emerged on the shoulder of the old county highway, with several of the men bleeding from small cuts on their faces and hands. Mr. Bellamy was in the worst shape. He looked like he had been attacked by a hundred angry cats. There was a trickle of blood running down his cheek and neck, into his shirt, which was ripped in several places. There was a big rip in his pants, just above the knee, and blood had soaked through the fabric all around it. He looked so miserable, Karen had to look away so he wouldn't see her laughing.

"It's not far now," she said. "See, you can see Pond Street from here."

"It's a good thing," the mayor grumbled. "I told everybody we'd meet at the high school at noon. We've got to head right over there, if we're going to make it on time."

Karen's face got very serious when she turned to Mr. Cross. "What are you going to tell them?" she asked. "Can you put the road in here? Will it work?"

Mr. Cross paused. "To tell you the truth, Karen, I don't know. It'll take some more work to see if this all makes sense. But there is one thing I do know. It looks too good to give up now. The project is back on."

Karen jumped into the air. "Yes," she shouted.

Chapter 34: Back in Business

As the group walked down Pond Street toward Karen's house, they looked a lot less polished than they had when they followed Karen out through the swamp two hours earlier. The men were dirty, scratched and ragged. Their khaki pants were dirty and torn. Mr. Bellamy was so tired, he was staggering. Only Karen and Ron looked fresh.

Her mother came to the door just as they approached. She had a nervous quizzical look on her face that changed to a broad smile when Karen ran to her.

"Mom, Mom," she yelled, "Mr. Cross says the project is back on. Isn't that great? They might be able to put a road around the swamp."

"That's fantastic," Mrs. Taylor said, still smiling, but shaking her head with wonder. "How did ..."

The mayor came over just then, interrupting her. "Excuse me, Mrs. Taylor. Are you coming to the meeting?"

"Yes, of course. I was only waiting for Karen."

"Good. I was hoping she could ride with you. There are some business matters the rest of us would like to discuss on the way."

"No problem. I'll just follow you."

The men got into the mayor's big car and drove off, while Karen and her mother followed.

"I wonder what they're talking about," Karen said suspiciously as they drove.

"Oh," said her mother, "there's probably lots to talk about now that the project is back on."

"Yeah, but it makes me nervous. Every time they talk business, something bad happens."

Her mother laughed. "You're not going to let them get away with anything, are you?"

"No way," Karen said seriously.

Her mother shook her head, with a slightly worried look in her eyes, but she didn't say anything.

They all walked into the gym together. The mayor asked Mrs. Taylor if Karen could come up on stage with the men. Karen wanted to shout, "No," but her mother said, "Sure." So Karen didn't get a vote.

The gym was packed. It looked like everyone in town was there. There was a quiet mutter going around the room, which quickly dropped into silence as Karen and the men went up on stage. The mayor went straight to the microphone.

"Well," he said, smiling out at a sea of expectant faces, "I'm glad to see so much interest in our little expedition. I'll just tell you that we found the old logging road right where Karen said it was, and we took it all the way around the swamp. You can see by our clothes it's kind of rough going, but you don't want to hear about our scratches and bruises. You want to hear what Mr. Cross is going to do about it. So, let's find out what he's got to say. Mr. Cross."

Mr. Cross walked up to the microphone as the mayor sat down.

"I won't keep you in suspense," he said. "That old logging road might be the solution we've all been hoping for. I can't say for sure until we've done some more work to make sure it's feasible, but it looks good so far, and it's certainly worth the trouble to find out. So, for now, the project is on."

Suddenly, the whole gym erupted in a spontaneous cheer. Mr. Cross let it go on for a full minute as he stood there and smiled out on all the happy people. Then he raised his arms and the cheering quickly stopped.

"Believe me, I'm just as happy as you are. Pine Springs is where we want our new Dew Drop bottling plant to be. And I just want to say one thing about that. One of the big reasons we want to be here is because you want us here. As we worked on the plans for our new plant, everything I heard from your mayor confirmed that you wanted us, in fact needed us, and would work hard to make a place for us here. That was very important to us, because Dew Drop is the kind of company that wants to be a part of the community where we make our home.

"When we thought we had come up against a wall and the project had to be cancelled, that was the reason I chose to come here and give you the bad news myself. Mayor Larson told me that word of the project had leaked out, and that the disappointment of having to cancel it might tear the town apart. That was the last thing I wanted. From everything I'd heard, Pine Springs was more than just a dot on the map. Pine Springs is a community, the kind of place where neighbors help neighbors and people depend on each other. You know that's more important than your crystal clear mountain water. It's more important than the big interstate highway that runs through your back yard. It would have been a terrible thing if our little project destroyed that.

"That's why I want to take this opportunity to recognize one of your neighbors that has done more for this project than anyone. She discovered our secret project before anyone, and from that moment, she has been with us every step of the way, reminding us what we have to do to make it work for your community. I know she's taken some heat – unfairly - for some of the decisions she's had to make along the way. I just want to tell you that everything she's done has helped to make this a better project – better for you, the citizens of Pine

223

Springs, and better for us, the Dew Drop Corporation. I hope you'll join me in thanking her – Karen Taylor."

Karen was so shocked, she just sat there with her mouth open when Mr. Cross turned to her and started clapping. Quickly, everyone in the audience began to clap too. A few people cheered. Karen thought she recognized her mother's voice, and maybe Davey Torvald's, too. She didn't know what to do. Finally, she stood up and nodded shyly to the crowd, then immediately sat down again.

When the cheering and clapping died down, Karen saw that there was one person in the crowd still standing. It was Mrs. Torvald. Mr. Cross didn't seem to know quite what to do, but he pointed to her and asked, "Do you have something you want to say?"

"Yes I do," she said loudly and firmly. The gym went perfectly silent. "I think there are quite a few people in this town who owe Karen and her mother a very big apology. I happen to know more of the wonderful things that Karen did for us on this project than any of you, and I also know of some of the disgraceful things that were done to her. When it looked like this environmental problem was going to stop the project, Karen and her mother were subjected to a campaign of social isolation that was shameful. You all know the part you played in that."

At that point, she looked down at her husband, whose shoulders were slumped forward as he sat in his chair and stared down at the floor. But she was not through. "Shame on all of us, but there was one individual who pushed us into this awful behavior, and he's sitting right there on that stage."

She pointed to the people sitting behind Mr. Cross. "You, Mr. Bellamy. You got my husband to spread the news about the project and Karen and the salamanders to the rest of the town, when it was supposed to be a secret. You told him to tell everyone to shun the Taylors. You specifically set out to punish them. You talk about tearing up the town – well, you did it on purpose, and I think that's disgraceful."

Mr. Cross started to say something, but he was interrupted when another person stood up. "That's right," he said loudly. It was a small man of about sixty, with gray hair, glasses and a thick white mustache, Mr. Colston, the man who owned the diner.

"They came to me and wanted me to fire Elaine Taylor. She is my best waitress and has always been very popular with my customers. I couldn't do that, and when I told them so, they threatened me with a boycott of my diner. I was very scared then, but now I'm only angry. Maybe an apology isn't even enough."

When Mr. Colston sat down, Mr. Cross looked furious. He turned to Mr. Bellamy. "Is this true?"

"I …" Mr. Bellamy shook his head and looked at the floor. His face, which had gradually grown as red as a fire engine, suddenly went white.

Mr. Cross made sure his next words were picked up by the microphone. "You're off this project from this minute on, and your boss is going to hear about this."

He turned to Karen. "Karen, let me be the first to apologize for the treatment you and your mother received. I assure you that, if I had known what Mr. Bellamy was up to, I never would have allowed it. But, since he was working on behalf of my company, I have to take responsibility for it. I promise you, it will never happen again."

Mr. Cross sat down and the mayor went back up to the microphone. The silence that greeted him was a sharp contrast to the applause of a few minutes before. "Karen," he said, turning to her. "I'm very sorry, and I'm probably even more responsible than Mr. Cross. I honestly don't know what we would have done on this project without you, and there's no way you should have had to put up with that kind of thing. So, for all the citizens of Pine Springs, let me say thank you and we're sorry."

There was another round of clapping, and then the mayor closed the meeting. "So that's it," he said, taking a deep breath. "We're back in business. From now on, there'll be no secrets on this project. I'll give an update to the *Pine Springs News* every week, and I'll call another meeting like this when there are any new and significant milestones to report. I want to thank you all for being here and join you in celebrating our good fortune."

Everyone crowded around Karen, shaking her hand, talking and smiling at her. A few apologized, and many seemed slightly embarrassed, but Karen answered them and smiled back as best she could. She just wanted to get out of there. These were the same people that wouldn't talk to her or even look at her just one day before. Karen could forgive them. She knew she would, but it couldn't happen quite this fast. As soon as she politely could, she found her mother and whispered, "Let's go home."

Her mother smiled a knowing smile and started edging through the crowd toward the door.

When they got home, Karen felt funny. It was the first time in what seemed like months that she didn't have something to worry about. She didn't say anything, but her mother somehow knew what Karen was feeling. She packed a picnic and they got in the car and drove up to Lookout Park.

When they were sitting at the rough table, eating their sandwiches and looking down at their town, Mrs. Taylor said, "You know Karen, you deserved all the nice things Mr. Cross said about you at the meeting today. You did something special."

Karen stared down at the green splotch of swamp, where she imagined the little pink and yellow spotted salamanders swimming and playing like they had for centuries. "I don't know. I didn't think it was so special. I thought I was just doing what anyone would do if they were in that situation."

Her mother thought about it for a minute. "I wish I believed that, but I don't. Not many kids would have done what you did, and no adult would have handled it that way."

"I don't know," Karen sighed. Then she suddenly sat up straighter. "Look down there," she said, pointing.

"What?"

"See that curving line where the woods are a little darker on the hillside. You can see it from here. That's the old logging road. There's nothing so special about what I did. It was right there in front of us all the time. I just pointed it out."

Her mother looked down and saw the faint outline of the old abandoned road curving along the hillside above the swamp. "You're right," she said, "but that's what's special. Most of us never see what's right in front of our noses."

Chapter 35: Visitors

Quite a few people came by the Taylor's house over the next few days to personally congratulate and thank Karen. A few were honest and strong enough to apologize for their part in the shunning, but many tried to pretend they'd had no part in it. By then, Karen had calmed down enough to receive them with polite and friendly smiles. She knew it was the "right" thing to do, though she didn't quite know why.

Two of the women who came by were strangers to Karen. Her mother seemed to know them, though. Mrs. Taylor brought out some iced tea and cookies and treated them like old friends as they offered warm words of praise and congratulations to Karen and her mother. When they left, Mrs. Taylor told Karen they were the same two who had made cutting remarks to her at the diner.

"How could you be so nice to them?" Karen asked, amazed and angry.

Her mother shrugged. "What's the point of holding a grudge? We've all got to live here. The way things worked out, now they feel like they've got to be nice to us. That's all I want from them, so I'm not going to do anything to change their minds. Anyway, isn't that what you're doing? These are the same people whose kids wouldn't talk to you."

"Yes, but I did something to make them hate me. You didn't."

"That doesn't make it any more worthwhile for me to keep hating them."

"I guess," Karen reluctantly agreed, "but sometimes it's hard not to."

"True."

That afternoon, she went over to the Gunderson's, expecting Mrs. Gunderson to send her home as usual, but she was surprised when Mrs. Gunderson instead took her into the living room, where Mr. Gunderson was sitting in his chair. He looked a little stronger than the last time she had seen him almost two weeks before. He still looked shriveled, but his color was better, and it didn't seem like such a strain for him to hold up his head. He was in a good mood, too.

"Hello, Karen," he said enthusiastically when Mrs. Gunderson announced her presence, "sit down. We've got a lot to talk about."

"We sure do," Karen laughed. "But how are you feeling? I've been pretty worried about you."

"I'm much better, thank you. For a while there, I wasn't sure I was going to make it, but I was so caught up in your struggle with the development project, I had to stick around to find out how it all came out. You know, I think it's the hard work and sacrifice to do things right that makes us strong. I heard the mayor recognized your contribution in front of the whole town and apologized for the silent treatment. That must make you feel pretty good."

"I guess so. I'm just happy that people will talk to me now, but I don't pay much attention to it. I know they could turn around and hate me again, just like that."

Mr. Gunderson sighed. "You're right. You can't put too much stock in what people think about you, one way or the other. If you're going to do that, you might as well be a politician, like the mayor."

"You know, I've been kind of wondering about him," Karen said. "At the meeting the other night, when they thought they had to give up on the new plant, the mayor and Mr. Bellamy weren't telling the truth about it. They made it seem like they were the ones that wanted to shut down the project when they heard about the salamanders. It wasn't that way at all."

"I know. That's the mayor's job. He wanted to put a nice face on it so that people wouldn't be angry with him. Remember, he's got to get elected again next year or he goes back to selling cars."

"You mean it's his job to lie?"

"Only when it's useful. And when he won't get caught."

"But he's the mayor. Shouldn't we be able to trust him?"

"That would be nice, I guess," Mr. Gunderson sighed, "but it's really more like the opposite. Most people don't expect him to tell the truth. I'm not sure they'd know what to do with him if he did – probably vote him out of office."

"Do you think he's a bad man?"

"Not particularly. I think he's a mayor and a politician. He's doing exactly what people expect him to do. They don't expect him to tell them the truth. That's not his job. Just like you shouldn't expect a corporation to consider the right and wrong of their business. It's not what they do.

"Anyway," he continued, "I have a confession to make. The mayor didn't come up with that lie. I did."

Karen was shocked. "You did? How? Why?"

"I felt awful about the way people were treating you when they found out that you warned the scientists about the new plant. I didn't want you to have to face that for as long as you lived in Pine Springs. Remember I told you I knew Mr. Bellamy's boss?"

"Yes."

"Well, I called him up and got him to tell me the name of their client – the Dew Drop Corporation. Then I called up Mr. Cross, the CEO of Dew Drop, and told him the situation. Dew

Drop sells juice drinks that they advertise as "natural." Harmony with nature is an important part of their corporate image. I suggested that Dew Drop might look like they were just another big corporation trampling the environment for their greedy purposes if it looked like it took a court order to get them to stop their project. On the other hand, they could show a strong environmental commitment by making it look like it was their decision to save the salamanders. It turned out I had no problem selling that idea to Mr. Cross. He immediately decided he wanted to come here and deliver the message himself. When he called the mayor to ask to be part of his meeting, the mayor was thrilled. It took some of the heat off him. So don't blame the mayor. If anyone is responsible for that lie, it's me and Mr. Cross. I don't think we're bad people, but we are business people, so we're very experienced at that kind of lying."

"You lied for me," Karen said softly.

"Yes."

"I always thought lying was wrong."

"Maybe it is. I don't know. In this situation, it seemed like the right thing, but ..." he shrugged, "I don't know."

"What about the rest of the project? It seemed like it was always going off in bad directions. Is that because other people did bad things, or were they just doing what they thought was right, too?"

"Karen, that's a very interesting question, one I've had a lot of time to think about. Here's what I think: The mayor may have broken the law if he asked Mr. Wilson to send out those letters to people on Pond Street who were behind on their mortgage payments. You see, he might have done that to help Mr. Bellamy's company, which is something an elected official isn't supposed to do. On the other hand, the reason he might have done something like that is because he thought it would help get the new plant built here in Pine Springs, something he thought would be very good for all of us. So, what do you think? Was that good or bad?"

"I don't know," Karen said thoughtfully. "It's sort of like you lying for me. Could it be a bad thing for good reasons?"

"Or a good thing for bad reasons. That's a very old question, and one I don't have an answer to. I don't think the mayor has anything to be proud of in all this. He let Mr. Bellamy run wild."

"What about Mr. Bellamy?" Karen persisted.

"What Mr. Bellamy did to get the town to shun you and your mother was very bad. If he really threatened Mr. Colston, that was illegal. I doubt if he'll get arrested, but it looks like he's going to pay a pretty big price for it. I talked to his boss yesterday and he wouldn't say what he's going to do, but I think Mr. Bellamy is going to have to find another line of work."

"Really?"

"I'd certainly fire him if he was working for me on a project that blew up the way this one did. "

"Is it my fault? I mean, is it because of what I did that he might get fired?"

"No, it's because of what he did. He was very sloppy and lazy in his work, and trying to take revenge on you and your mother was unforgiveable."

"I didn't mean to get him fired."

"No, but you did want to make sure that he didn't hurt anybody else – like the people on this street or the salamanders. And you didn't want to be hurt either. But when he thought you were getting in his way, he wanted to hurt you. Believe me, he deserves whatever punishment he gets."

Karen was silent for a moment, thinking about it. Finally, she shook her head. "It's very strange."

Mr. Gunderson laughed out loud. "Yes it is. But remember, you're the only one who sees how strange it really is. The rest of us think of it as business as usual."

The visits from neighbors became a strain for Karen. She felt like her face was going to crack from smiling so much. But there was one visit that made all the rest worthwhile.

It was Sunday afternoon, and Karen's mom had just come home from the diner. Karen was doing some dishes, while her mother changed out of her uniform. When the doorbell rang, Mrs. Taylor walked through the front room, saying she'd get it. Karen heard her mother greet their visitor and there was a funny catch in her voice, like she was surprised. There was something familiar about the visitor's voice, too, but Karen couldn't hear him distinctly enough to know who it was. She dried her hands and went to the door.

Ron was standing on the front step. He was wearing khaki pants and a blue shirt with a pattern of thin gray lines running through it. He was smiling, and Karen noticed the laughing eyes that reminded her of her father. Her mother stood in the doorway, smiling uncertainly, as if she didn't know quite what to do with him.

"Hello, Karen," he said when he saw her. "I just wanted to stop by to thank you for what you did for the salamanders. Janice's paper got accepted by one of the big journals, and Mr. Cross has agreed to turn the swamp over to the state. It will be protected wetlands from now on."

"Wow," Karen said. "That's great. Come on in. You met my mom, right?"

"Well, yes – just now." Ron followed Karen over to the sitting area, where she gave him the comfortable chair. Her mother came along and sat next to Karen on the couch. Karen noticed that she seemed unusually quiet, and she forgot the iced tea, which was part of the ritual for these visits. Karen eagerly ran over to the kitchen to get it. While she filled a tray with tea, glasses, ice, sugar, lemon, cookies and napkins, she listened to the awkward conversation between Ron and her mother.

"Karen was very helpful, Mrs. Taylor," Ron said. "She helped us find the salamanders and then she helped catch Newton, the first one we examined in the lab. As you probably know she also helped me start the process of getting the swamp protected. I know that was a tough decision for her, and she must have taken a lot of grief for it."

"Yes she did," Mrs. Taylor said seriously, "but I was wondering how she happened to meet you?"

"Just by accident, I guess. I was helping the surveyor do a map of the site for the new plant, and Karen was out there walking around in the woods."

"You were working with the surveyor? I thought you were a scientist."

Ron laughed. "That would be a generous term for it. I'm in a graduate program down at the state university. The surveyor work helps me pay the rent."

"Oh, you're still a student. I thought you were older." Karen's mom sounded slightly flustered.

"I'm 36," Ron said. "I worked for awhile after college before I decided to go back."

"I'm sorry. If it's not fair to ask a woman her age, I guess it's not fair to ask a man either."

"No problem, Mrs. Taylor. Sometimes I feel a little too old to be in school myself."

"Oh, no. I didn't mean that. But please call me Elaine. I noticed that Karen calls you by your first name, so I was thinking ... um, would it be alright if I call you Ron?"

"That would be fine."

Karen brought the tray over and set it on the coffee table. "There," she said, "some nice iced tea and cookies to celebrate the good news."

"What news?" her mother asked, confused.

"About Ron's paper and the swamp."

"Of course. That's wonderful." Mrs. Taylor seemed slightly embarrassed.

"Karen, it's so different to see you at home serving tea so elegantly," Ron said to fill the silence. "I'm used to seeing you out in the woods in your hiking boots."

"I think that's more the real me. Mom says I got it from my dad. He loved the woods."

"Did he take you hiking a lot?"

"I don't think so. I was too little when he died."

"Oh, I'm sorry. I didn't know he was dead."

"That's alright. It was a long time ago."

"What about you, Ron?" Karen's mom asked. "Do you have any kids?"

"No. I've never been married."

"Why? Is science your only love?"

"No, no," Ron laughed. "I think I'm more like Karen. I just like to spend time in the woods and swamps. Studying biology is a way to get out there."

"Well, it's great that you've gone so far with your education. I always tell Karen to go as far in school as she can, so she doesn't end up a dumb waitress like me."

"Being a waitress doesn't make you dumb," Ron said seriously, "just like being a PhD doesn't make you smart."

"It can't hurt, though."

"That's true. Most of the dumb PhDs I know were dumb before they started."

"You know what I mean."

"Yes, I do, and you're absolutely right. Karen, listen to your mother. Always do your best in school, and take it as far as you can."

"I will," Karen said, rolling her eyes comically.

"Alright," Ron laughed. "I guess you don't need to hear it from me, too."

Karen noticed that Ron picked just that moment to look over at her mother, who was looking back at him. There was some meaning in their glance that Karen didn't understand, but it didn't make her suspicious or angry. It made her glad.

Ron didn't stay much longer, but as he was leaving, he mentioned that he would be coming back to the swamp regularly to study Newton and his friends.

"Great," Karen said. "Can I help?"

"Sure."

"Okay, then stop by here the next time you're going out in the swamp. Any time."

Ron looked to Karen's mother.

"Yes, Ron. Please stop by whenever you're in the neighborhood," she said, smiling warmly.

"Thank you, Elaine. I will."

Chapter 36: It All Works Out

The next day was Monday of the last week of school. Karen got to the bus stop early, as she usually did. For the first time in weeks, the other kids smiled at her, but they didn't seem to have anything to say. Karen thought it must be hard for them to talk to her after they hadn't for so long. Davey was practicing handstands with Matt Talbot. When the bus came, Karen got on and took her usual seat, sliding over next to the window. Normally, the seat next to her would have remained empty the whole way to school, but not that day. Davey walked down the aisle and sat down next to her.

"Hi," he said.

"Hi."

All the kids were watching, but Davey didn't pay any attention. He sat rigidly and stared straight ahead.

"Can you talk now?" Karen asked.

"Yeah. My dad says it's alright … now," Davey said bitterly. "My mom made him."

"You mean he wouldn't let you before?"

"No. He said you stabbed us in the back and if he caught me talking to you, I'd get a whipping. It doesn't matter. I never should have listened to him. I wanted to talk to you the whole time."

"Really?"

"Yeah, I did. I knew you'd make it come out okay in the end, and I told him that, but he wouldn't listen. He was so angry."

"I guess he had something to be angry about."

"He's always angry, and he's always wrong. I'm never going to listen to him again."

"Don't do that. He's your father."

"I don't care. I don't think my mother will ever listen to him, either." Davey scowled and went silent.

The kids a few rows away, who hadn't overheard what they were talking about, probably thought he was mad at Karen again. Some of them might have wondered if the silent treatment was back on. But then, why was he sitting with her?

After riding in silence for a few minutes, Karen said, "Don't be mad, Davey. It's all over."

"I know," Davey sighed, "but it wasn't right. I've got to learn how to think for myself, like the way you do."

Karen felt a small burst of pride at the unconscious admiration in Davey's voice. "I think you've already learned," she said.

"You do?"

"Uh-huh. You wouldn't be sitting here, talking to me, if you hadn't."

Davey's scowl relaxed into a thoughtful expression. "Maybe you're right," he said, and he seemed surprised and pleased, too.

The school day wasn't bad. Everybody was like the kids at the bus stop. They smiled and they wanted to be nice to Karen, but they couldn't think of anything to say. After weeks of being coldly ignored, that was good enough for Karen. It was weird, but at least it was moving in the right direction. Maybe things would settle down to normal again someday.

After school was even better. Meg Carol sat with her on the bus. It was a little awkward at first, but Meg was nice. She apologized for the weeks of silence that Karen had had to endure and confirmed some things that Karen had suspected. Most of the kids didn't even understand what they were doing. They just went along. Davey had been one of the first.

Naturally, the kids had noticed, but Davey had never pushed them to follow. In fact, he wouldn't talk about it at all. If anyone mentioned Karen to him, he got angry.

"I think he likes you," Meg said.

Despite herself, Karen blushed. "What do you mean?" she asked, to cover her confusion.

"You know," Meg giggled.

When Karen got home, she changed out of her school clothes and spread her books out on the table. The teachers weren't giving much homework, since there were only three more days of school left. She planned to quickly get it done and take a nice long tromp in the woods, but it didn't work out that way.

She couldn't seem to concentrate. The silly idea that Meg Carol had planted in her head kept spinning around and around, getting her lost in a lot of dizzy daydreams. It was a silly idea because she and Davey were just friends. It couldn't be anything else. Davey was popular and older, and she was unpopular and not even very pretty. It was just because they lived close to each other and Davey was a nice, outgoing kind of boy. It couldn't be anything more than that, could it?

Ten minutes passed and all she'd done was put her name and the date on a piece of paper. That's when there was a knock at the door. Karen looked at the paper and shook her head, frowning. At this rate, she'd never make it out of sixth grade. She went to the door and found Davey standing on her front step.

"Um, hi," he said.

"Hi," Karen said, conscious that a blush was trying to creep up into her cheeks.

"You doing anything?"

"No, I um … No."

"You want to hang out?"

"Okay."

"What do you want to do?"

"I don't know. What do you want to do?"

"I don't know. Maybe we could ride bikes, or something."

"No. You know what? I was just going to do my homework and take a walk in the woods. The homework can wait. You want to go for a walk? You know, if they get the okay, construction is going to start in just a few weeks. After that, it'll never be the same."

"Yeah, okay," Davey agreed easily.

They went out and sat on the flat rock, which was bathed in warm sunshine. The swamp lay before them, dark and cool and peaceful. Karen felt like she loved it more every time she saw it. Maybe it was the cute little salamanders that lived down there. Maybe it was the pride she felt for helping to save them. Or maybe it was just the swamp itself, so dignified and eternal. It was always the same. It gave her a sense of security and strength, a base to help her face all the confusion and weirdness in the world beyond.

"It's beautiful, isn't it," she said.

"What is?" Davey asked.

"The swamp."

"Oh. Yeah, I guess so." Davey was thinking of something else.

They sat in silence and sunshine for awhile, Karen gazing down into the swamp, Davey on his back, staring up into the sky.

"How did you know what to do?" he asked.

"When?"

"You know, all along – about the new plant and all that?"

"I didn't. I just did what I thought was right at the time. Mr. Gunderson helped me with the business stuff."

"I wish I could understand stuff like that," Davey said.

"I didn't say I understood it," Karen said. "It's the adult world, and they don't think like we do. We probably can't ever understand it until we're adults, and I'm not sure we should even want to."

"Yeah, but you got into it and did something, something even the adults had to accept. Most kids can't do that."

"Oh, I don't know. We can do more than we think we can."

"You can, but that's because you're smarter and more sure of yourself."

"Sure of myself?" Karen laughed. "I haven't been sure about anything in this whole mess."

"But sure enough to do something about it," Davey argued. "That's what I want. I want to be able to do something, you know, something important, like what you did."

"You will. I know you will."

"You really think so?"

Karen looked at him and suddenly realized that she really did think he would do something important someday. He wasn't particularly smart, but he was honest, and he really was starting to think for himself. "I'm almost sure of it," she said with conviction.

"Wow," he said as he lay back to look at the sky some more.

A little later he said, "Are you going to be around this summer?"

"Where else would I go?"

"I don't know. Matt's going to Minnesota to visit with his cousins. I thought you might be doing something like that."

"I don't have any cousins."

"Well, then maybe we can hang out some more. I'm not going anywhere, either."

"I'd like that," Karen said.

"Me too."

That night was Mrs. Taylor's night off. She was home fixing dinner while Karen did her neglected homework.

"Guess who stopped into the diner this morning," she said, trying to sound casual.

"Who?" Karen asked. She could hear the excitement in her mother's voice.

"Mr. Cross, the head of the Dew Drop company. He sat at the counter and we had a nice chat."

"Yeah?" Karen knew there was more to it than that.

"Yeah, and he said I could get a job at the new plant next year. He guaranteed it."

"Really? That's great."

"I know. I told him I don't know anything but waitressing, but he said that wouldn't be a problem. They have lots of training programs, and not only that but I could take courses at the Community College. The company would even pay for them. What do you think about that?"

"I think it's fantastic."

"You don't think I'm too old to go back to school?"

"No way. You're not any older than Ron, and he's still in school."

"That's true," Mrs. Taylor said thoughtfully.

She tore open a box of spaghetti and slid the noodles into a big pan of boiling water. As the water started to boil again, she stirred up the noodles to keep them from sticking together. "Do you think he thought I was dumb?" she asked.

Karen had been working on her math. "Who?" she asked. "You mean Mr. Cross?"

"No, I mean Ron. Was he just being nice, and he really thinks I'm just a dumb waitress?"

"He better not. No, I'm sure he didn't. Anyway, you don't act or sound like a dumb anything. Like he said, you can be a brilliant waitress or a dumb professor."

"Well, just the same, I'd like to feel a little more educated."

"That's what I keep telling you," Karen laughed. "You should take it as far as you can."

After dinner, Karen was helping her mother with the dishes.

"Well, I guess that Townsend outfit isn't going to buy our house now," her mother said.

"No."

"The money would have been nice, but I'm glad."

"Me too," Karen said. "I like our little house."

"I do too, and you know I never wanted to move."

"Me either."

"That reminds me. I'm going over to the bank tomorrow and give Mr. Wilson that money we got for the Purchase and Sale agreement. That will almost get us up to date with our payments."

"How much was that?" Karen asked.

"Two thousand, nine hundred and fifty dollars."

"And how much did we owe?"

"Three thousand."

"Huh," Karen said as if she was surprised.

She went to the cupboard and took down the jar where she had deposited all those dollar bills from her job reading to Mr. Gunderson. She dumped them out on the table. "There's the other fifty dollars," she said, smiling proudly. "See Mom, I told you it would all work out."

Made in the USA
Middletown, DE
17 May 2022

65823666R00139